M.B Stevenson

Memorials of the Rev. John Frederick Stevenson

M.B Stevenson

Memorials of the Rev. John Frederick Stevenson

ISBN/EAN: 9783337092931

Printed in Europe, USA, Canada, Australia, Japan

Cover: Foto ©Andreas Hilbeck / pixelio.de

More available books at **www.hansebooks.com**

From a Photo by Martin & Sallnow, 416, Strand, London, W.C.

MEMORIALS

OF THE REV.

JOHN FREDERICK STEVENSON,

B.A., LL.B., D.D.

BY HIS WIFE.

London:

JAMES CLARKE & Co., 13 & 14, Fleet Street.

MDCCCXCI.

IN MEMORIAM, J. F. S.

By his cousin, Joseph Truman. First published in the London "Spectator."

A LIFE from our impoverished life has past,
  Gentle, and pure, and free;
A soldier in the camp of light, right-fast,
  With old-world chivalry:

A mind that frank, alert, inquisitive,
  Kept a saint's ardour still,
Whose dauntless searching for the truths that live,
  Left no agnostic chill.

Mourn we no more, 'twere wisest, and 'twere well
  With the world's hope to blend;
What matters now the painful cloud that fell,
  And settled on the end!

O'er breathing earth, and through the moving air,
  A force resurgent rolls;
In realms invisible arises fair
  The Easter of all souls.

One day for us the sombre veil will lift;
  A mighty light shall flow;
And we no longer question, doubt, and drift,
  And fear, but find and know!

PREFACE.

IN publishing these "Memorials" my thanks are due to the Rev. J. Jackson Goadby, of Henley-on-Thames, for his aid in correcting the proofs. By the desire of many friends, extracts from the memorial sermons and addresses delivered in Reading, Montreal, and Brixton, are included. I have also added a few of the many letters received after Dr. Stevenson's death which may be of use in revealing something of his character; or may prove consoling and helpful to others who, like myself, have suffered in this sore bereavement.

M. B. STEVENSON.

MONTREAL, *July*, 1891.

CONTENTS.

SERMONS.

ETHICAL.

viii CONTENTS.

JOHN FREDERICK STEVENSON was the eldest son of the Rev. John Stevenson, M.A., for many years the earnest and devoted pastor of the Borough Road Baptist Church, London. His grandfather, the Rev. Thomas Stevenson, was a contemporary of Robert Hall, whom he well knew and whom in many points he resembled. He was a man of unusual talent and pulpit eloquence; a sturdy Puritan of the old type, in the days when a man had to suffer for his nonconformity. An amusing story is told of him and his relation to a neighbouring clergyman who also bore the name of Stevenson. In those days clergymen were not always appointed because of their fitness for the sacred office; and, if report is to be trusted, the dignitary in question conferred no honour upon his profession. Perhaps the near neighbourhood of a hard-working "dissenting brother" proved a source of irritation to a man of more secular pursuits; but certain it is that Thomas Stevenson found no favour in the eyes of his ecclesiastical namesake. Particularly he resented his use of the

2

prefix " Reverend " ; and one day a letter intended for the nonconforming Thomas falling into his hands, he sent it to its rightful owner with the accompanying note :—

" Sir,—If you had not assumed a title to which you had no right, this mistake would never have occurred."

No notice was taken of the insult at the time ; but some months later a pile of manuscript sermons, prepared for the use of those unhappy preachers who are unable to compose discourses of their own, having been purchased for his own requirements by the clergyman, were sent by mistake to Thomas Stevenson. The opportunity for retaliation proved irresistible ; and one can imagine the grim smile with which they were packed up and remitted to their proper owner with the enclosure :—

" Sir,—If *you* had not assumed a title to which you had no right, *this* mistake would never have occurred."

But those old days, we are glad to believe, have passed away for ever. It was the happy experience of the subject of this memorial to find the only rivalry between himself and clergymen of the Established Church one of love and of good works. This was pre-eminently the case during his life in Canada, where the Church is free from the fetters of State patronage and control.

John Frederick Stevenson was born at Lough-boro', in 1833. While still an infant the family removed to London, his father, the Rev. John Stevenson, having been invited to become pastor of the Borough Road Baptist Church. Travelling in those days was by coach; and a long journey it proved for the young mother and babe. The little one, however, thrived in his new surroundings, and found in South London a congenial home. Here he was brought up, and ever after loved it with that mysterious devotion which a true Londoner feels for those "long, unlovely streets," half hidden, as Ruskin has it, "with the modern mystery of smoke." I remember being struck with this in reading the life of Charles Dickens. Even in the midst of the loveliest scenery of Switzerland, he occasionally breaks out into a home-sick cry for London; longing for a prowl around the old haunts, peopled for him with a life so fantastic, yet so real.

"Fred," as he was familiarly called as a lad, grew up a somewhat dreamy boy, never so happy as when sitting in a quiet corner with a book; and if the book were on some abstract subject, so much the better for his enjoyment. Much of his early education was gained in a garret of his London home, where volumes from an old library were stored. Here he feasted upon Berkeley, Paley, and other theologians; but above all, and perhaps best of all for his English education, Shakespeare, Milton, Goldsmith, Spencer, here unfolded their magic pages and filled him with delight. His memory at this youthful period was "wax to receive and marble to retain," and the contents of the garret library proved a precious possession for ever. In after-years, when deeply interested in educational questions, he was especially anxious that the study of English literature should form an important and systematic part of school training. He felt that his " garret culture " was of the greatest personal benefit to him throughout his life, and helped largely to that training of the tongue and of the ear so necessary to a public man. " I would have the youth of England saturated with the classical writers of their own tongue, just as the Greeks were with Greek," he would say. He received his general training at University College, London, under the well-known professors, Francis Newman, Malden, and De Morgan. In 1850 he became a student at the Baptist College, Stepney (now Regent's Park), for his theological course, under Dr. Angus, and finished this part of his career by taking his B.A. at the London University. Among his fellow-students were Charles Vince, Samuel Cox, Clement Bailhache, and Luscombe and Henry Hull; and with them he formed friendships which only death has dissolved. " His Sunday services," says a college friend, " were in constant demand, even in those early days. His preaching from the first was marked with great fluency, a happy choice of diction, and occasional incisiveness, all infused with a quiet glow of emotion—parts sparkling with satirical play." He possessed, like his father and grandfather, a natural eloquence, and had the advantage of being trained in elocution by Sheridan Knowles, who sometimes, when his patience was tried by less satisfactory pupils, would turn to Fred Stevenson and say, " Come up here, my dear, and show them how to do it!" While at Stepney, when not engaged in preaching himself, he often had the opportunity of hearing some of the best London ministers. Howard Hinton and Baldwin Brown were his special favourites. Two widely different men, but both useful to the young student, in forming his own standard of pulpit taste and excellence. To the teaching of the latter, indeed, he was indebted all through his after-life. On one occasion, while listening to his celebrated sermon " The way home," Mr. Brown apologizing for exceeding his time, his enthusiastic young hearer audibly exclaimed, " Go on!" Fortunately he was sitting near the pulpit; the preacher saw how it was, and smiled kindly at the eager face upturned to his own. How little either of them could have guessed that one day the unknown young student would become the successor of the prominent minister, whose career was then in its prime. His twenty-first birthday found him the pastor of his first charge at Long Sutton, Lincolnshire—sitting in rather lonely dignity in his own study, missing the home faces and birthday greetings, which he was not too old to appreciate. Writing to his father he says :—

"I have made this day a season of new resolutions and fervent hopes and prayers. May God give me His gracious assistance that my now commencing manhood be consecrated to Him. There is much here to be done in His cause, and I only hope it may be accomplished in His fear and for His glory. The friends have received me with very great kindness. They do not appear to have been efficiently supplied of late, and the cause is in a poor state. . . . I preached in the evening from the words of Jesus, 'I will come and heal him,' as applied to the poor paralytic. The congregation was very attentive and quite double the usual number. Is not this so far encouraging?"

The four years he spent at Long Sutton seem, on the whole, to have been happy ones. His salary was about eighty pounds a year—not quite so humble as that of Goldsmith's village pastor, though, like him, his wants were few. He seems to have felt quite a man of means, however, and writes amusingly to his mother of his independence :—

"My expenses average about eight-and-sixpence or nine shillings a week. Several friends have been to see me, and I have invited more than one to spend the evening. The sense of having a perfect right to do so" (he had formerly been lodging with a family where this was impossible), "and of welcoming my visitors to a table all my own, is exceedingly pleasant."

He was inclined to look on the bright side of everything, as indeed who should not at the age of twenty-one?

Here, he says, he preached his "wild-oat" sermons, and the people were kind and patient with him, giving him time for thought and mental development. He always regarded it as a misfortune for a young man to begin his ministry in a prominent church. The quieter the better for the first few years, he said, so that the "'prentice hand" should get practice before he attempted great things.

Unfortunately in Long Sutton Mr. Stevenson's physical health fared not so well as his mental condition. In those days, before the draining of the fens, to live in Lincolnshire meant to be a martyr to ague, and to this rule he was no exception; indeed he suffered from it so severely that it affected his constitution for many years afterwards.

In 1858 Mr. Stevenson accepted an invitation to the Mansfield Road Church, Nottingham, where his old friend and fellow-student, the Rev. Dr. Cox, author of "Salvator Mundi" and other works, afterwards succeeded him. He was at first co-pastor with the Rev. G. A. Syme, M.A., a gentleman of some repute amongst the General Baptists; but on

his retirement through ill-health, Mr. Stevenson
assumed the entire pastorate.   Soon after his
settlement he married Priscilla, daughter of Mr.
King, of Boston, and life seemed to open out full of
promise for the future.   Like a bolt out of a clear
sky, however, a crushing sorrow was about to befal
him.   After fifteen months of happiness his young
wife, who had left him in the morning in perfect
health, was brought home at noon, a corpse.   After
rather rapid walking she had fallen in the street,
and instantly expired; heart disease, unsuspected
even by herself, being the cause of her death.
Out of the shadow of this bitter bereavement
the young minister emerged, not only with a deeper
experience of human suffering, but with a deeper
sympathy for all sufferers—a sympathy which was
a large factor in making him so greatly beloved by
his people in his after-ministry.   The roots of his
sorrow went down deep into his life, and bore fruit
not only in his private, but in his public ministra-
tions.   It was as an anointing of the Lord which
enabled him to speak "a word in season to the
weary," and to apply the comfort wherewith he
also had been comforted of God to bowed and
broken hearts.

Like most people, however, with a deep sense of
the pathos of life, he was keenly alive to the
ludicrous, and sometimes found it difficult to
refrain from a smile where it would have been
misunderstood or unseemly.   Preaching on one

occasion at an anniversary service, a large dog strolled up the centre aisle with slow deliberation, and planted himself as an auditor a few paces from the pulpit, from whence he looked up into the preacher's face with such serious attention that he altogether imperilled his gravity. Fortunately the sexton succeeded in removing the interloper before the situation had grown too embarrassing. But it was frequently his experience that a quick sense of humour, while adding to the amusement of the man was painfully upsetting to the minister.

About this time he began to feel the difficulty of his position as a General Baptist. While attached to many individuals amongst them, he was some-what cramped and fettered by the smallness of the denomination. It must not be supposed that he objected to the rite of " believer's baptism "; as long as he lived he maintained that, should any unbaptized converts desire it, he was perfectly willing to admit them into the Church by immersion. He could not, however, feel the *form* to be of the signal importance with which many, even of his own congregation, invested it; and when pressed for more definite sermons on the subject doctrinally, he found it distasteful to comply. Forms of all kinds were irksome to him. During his residence at Long Sutton he had lived, for the most part, in the house of a godly Quaker family, and had, almost unconsciously, been influenced by their views. He enjoyed the simplicity of their services;

and the "Friends' Meeting," which he sometimes attended, was a source of much spiritual benefit to him. In this connection he was fond of quoting from Thomas Lynch's quaint and suggestive poem "A church with bells" :—

> "I went the silent Friends to see,
>   And there no bells could ring;
> For how could any music be
>   Where nobody would sing?
> But as we all were sitting hushed,
>   Up rose a sister grey,
> And said, with face a little flushed,
>   'This is a sunny day,
> And Jesus is our inward light
>   To guide us on our way.'
> 'Ah yes,' said I, 'this sister pure,
>   The old, glad tidings tells;
> And here too, I am very sure,
>   I've found a church with bells.'"

He was in much sympathy also with Bushnell's "Christian Nurture," which he read at this period. The organic unity of the family, which should result in the children of Christian parents being brought up as Christians—"no more Christians with families, but Christian families," as Bushnell says, seemed to him reasonable and Scriptural.

Coming into contact with the Rev. Paxton Hood (with whom he afterwards enjoyed a lifelong friendship), Mr. Stevenson intimated his willingness to accept an invitation to a Congregational church, and was shortly after called to the pastorate of

Trinity Chapel, Reading. This was a change which he never had reason to regret. Pastor and people soon became warmly attached to each other, and as long as he lived the memory of his ministry among them was cherished as one of his most sacred and tender recollections.

He went to Reading in 1863, in the thirtieth year of his age. His views had ripened and settled into what I may call a " Broad Evangelicalism." Indeed a friend, laughingly accusing him of his "breadth," was answered, " Broad, if you like, but I do not give up the word 'evangelical'; it is too good to be parted with."

The essence of his sermons might be condensed in the teaching " that God was in Christ, reconciling the world unto Himself." " What men find it so difficult to realize," he would say, " is, that God loves them. They will believe in Him as Judge, as King, as Governor, condemning or approving, pleased or displeased ; but what they do not see is that the love of God is the strongest, deepest fact in the universe. If they did it would prove irresistible. Christ is the great Revealer of the heart of God. The attraction is there, and must go on ; as He has said, ' I, if I be lifted up, will draw all men unto Me.' "

What he himself said of Professor Elmslie, in an article written shortly after his death, was equally true of the writer : " He was not satisfied with a partial or merely logical view of any of the great doctrines of the gospel. He delighted to look at them from different sides, and to set them in various points of light. His teaching was eminently constructive. There was no tendency in his mind to rejection for the sake of novelty or change. He was probably more keenly alive to the presence of truth under varied forms than eager to overthrow any mode of thought which has ever yielded nourishment to the spiritual life of earnest and godly men. Hence he was popular with men of different mental tendencies, although entirely candid and fearlessly outspoken. . . . He looked forward to fuller truth as the result of wider investigation. He did not expect to destroy, or even innovate, but perpetually to add; and saw in the theology he loved so well the grandest gymnastic of the human mind, as well as a majestic vestibule of the temple of God."

As time went on, and he grew to be a power in the denomination, it might have been said of him, as has been said of another whose position much resembled his own, "that his part became very much that of the Reconciliationist—the man who is the intermediary between the new *cultus* and the old faith."

On the platform he was perhaps an almost greater power than in the pulpit. Always diffident, it seemed as if he needed the first round of applause to put him thoroughly *en rapport* with his audience; once being assured of their sympathy, everything became possible to him, and he carried his listeners with him to the close. I have often felt that in the pulpit, if he could have been permitted to hear an expression of the feeling of the congregation it would have been an immense help to him. He was more destitute of the quality which, for want of a better word, I may call "assurance," than any public man I ever knew, and hence had none of the pardonable pleasure which so many are able to take in their own performances. The utmost he ever said, even when most happy in his public utterances, was that "he had been able to speak with comfort."

The occasion of his first coming prominently before the Reading public was when, soon after his arrival in the town, an indignation meeting was held by the Nonconformists to protest against the insult offered them by the late Bishop Wilberforce, who in a recent charge had classed them with " bad cottages and beer-shops" as " hindrances to the clergy." The Rev. John Aldis and other of the leading ministers spoke, and the new-comer electri-fied his audience with a speech of so much fire and brilliance that every one was asking who the young man was.

A Liberal in politics, he did good work for his colleagues, and was a great support to Mr. Shaw Lefevre, at that time M.P. for Reading.

In the year following his removal to Reading, he married Miss Davis, daughter of Dr. Davis, secretary of the Religious Tract Society. The union was a singularly happy one, and she who writes these imperfect pages can only thank God that so many years of life and work together were granted to them. It is a delicate, and to her an impossible, task, to lift the veil that hides the sacredness of their domestic life. Enough to say that it was in the home that both gained strength for outside toil, and felt the cares that infest a public life soothed and quieted and forgotten. In Reading their five children—three boys and two girls—were born to them, each new inmate adding to the happiness of their home.

One or two extracts from Mr. Stevenson's letters will be the best interpreters of his life at this period. It should be said, however, that he never was a ready writer; and his letters are always as much as possible condensed. He disliked the act of writing, maintaining that it cramped his thoughts as much as his movements.

Owing to this, it was years after his ministry began before he took any but the briefest notes into the pulpit. And it was always true of him that his best sermons were extemporaneous; though, as he himself would admit, with a shrug of his shoulders, "so are my worst." As time went on, however, he grew to feel that the written sermon struck a more certain average—not always rising so high, but sure of not falling so low, as one simply thought out might do.

When first called to Reading he says, writing to his mother :—

" My first Sunday here is now past. I have to be thankful for a *very* cordial welcome on the part of my new friends, and for much comfort in preaching yesterday. The chapel was well filled at both services, and I believe that what I said has fallen on ' good ground.' My own view of my prospects is that they were never, on the whole, so good, and though I look forward to difficulties of many kinds (as who is without them ?), yet I put my trust in God for wisdom and skill to conquer them. I am anxious above all things to do God's work in His way, and I thank Him for placing me where, so far as I can judge, there is every prospect of my working with an affectionate and congenial people. May He fulfil my hopes for His name's sake ! "

That these hopes were abundantly realized is evident from the fact that under his leadership the Church became too strait for the congregation, and was enlarged to seat half as many again.

To his father he writes :—

" I won't enter now at large on any metaphysical or theological discussions. But I am intensely interested in the processes of mind by which your original views of the will have modified of late. Your method of investigation is surely unimpeachable. The exact vein itself into which you have finally settled I do not quite know. It will come out probably more easily in talk than in correspondence, and I long for a conversation. My philosophical studies lately have had reference to two things: the nature of what we call "matter," so far as knowable; and Mr. Grove's doctrine of the Correlation of Forces (or, as Herbert Spencer calls it, the 'Persistence of Force'). These are rather two aspects of one subject than wholly distinct. The tendency of my studies seems to be to overthrow realism. Matter fades into force, and force into connection in reason, *i.e.*, into quantitative or mathematical relations. For so much emotion which disappears, a constantly related quantity or intensity of heat (or electricity, or light, or chemical force, or all) appears. This seems to be what we mean by causation in nature. More when we meet."

To his mother he writes shortly after the birth of his first child :—

" The boy grows daily, and twines himself about our hearts wonderfully. Poor little fellow, launched all unconscious on this strange journey of life, am I glad to see him or no? Well, yes, I am; and yet it is no unmixed joy. It is a terrible thing to live, after all. I am afraid that is the lesson most of us learn from the experience of years. To be a human being is to be an actor in a tragi-comic drama, of which the tragedy is by far the larger part. What it all means he would be a very shallow theorist who should dare to say. I don't want to write gloomily, however, you have need of something else than that. My daily and hourly prayer is that God may guide and bless you."

From this last extract it will be seen that "the burden of the mystery" weighed upon him at times, as it does upon all thoughtful minds. At this period of his life, however, he was generally cheerful, except when suffering from the much-dreaded "bilious-nervous" headaches, which too often made Monday a day of misery to him. His health was never so good as his friends generally imagined; and much of his work was done under the tension of suffering to which he would allow no reprieve.

Though truly devout, he had nothing of the prig or "goody-good young man" in his composition. The following extract, written about this time to a young minister who was also an intimate friend, will, I trust, be pardoned as revealing the genuine fun and naturalness of his early manhood.

"My DEAR F.,—I am very glad the B.'s have had the good sense and good feeling to elect you. The eight or nine elderly feminines who differ, will not, I hope, break your heart, though you are in some danger of breaking theirs. As you say, with a touch of wisdom beyond your tender years, a little personal attention will convert them quickly, and perhaps suddenly. The only danger is lest they should become too demonstratively affectionate !

"I am more than glad to have you so near. *'Gloria in excelsis!'* We shall have a chance of

3

long walks and talks together, which will do *me* good, whatever be their effect upon *you*. I have no doubt you will build up the church, and when you get to know the people I am sure you will find a good deal of spiritual life and mental movement among them. (Mark the alliteration!) You are right in taking a holiday, and to settle it beforehand.

"I shall be very glad to know your parents, and hope I may see them in May. They must be capital people, judging from their descendant! Especially so if you remember the '*nos nequiores*' of the poet."

If I were asked to give a definition of his character in two words, they would be "simplicity" and "sympathy." He was always transparent and sincere as a child; "hoping all things and believing all things" of those with whom he came into contact. His power of throwing himself into the thought and feeling of others was remarkable. He literally rejoiced with those who rejoiced and wept with those who wept. I remember hearing the late James Hinton remark, "that our sympathy with other people was never likely to be keen enough to hurt ourselves"; and, generally speaking, he may be right, but Mr. Stevenson certainly proved an exception to this rule. Indeed the doctor's verdict at last was, that he had worn himself out by the keenness of his emotions, and injured the delicate brain and nerves past recovery.

A letter written after his settlement in Canada to a beloved friend in England on hearing of the death of his wife, will illustrate what I have said. It should be mentioned that "Millie," of whom he speaks so tenderly, had grown up in his Reading church, and was much endeared to him by many old associations.

To H. W. S. Worsley-Benison, Esq.*

"My dearest H.,—This is most dreadful. Arthur's letter has just come in, and given us this great grief as the news from home. Oh, my poor, dear Millie! almost my child, and always most dearly and tenderly beloved! And you, H., my poor boy; how well I know it—that utter, hopeless, wasting desolation, which dries up the very springs of life and shuts out peace and joy. I would give I know not what to be with you—to cross the great ocean and come to you—and yet if I were there I could not do the only thing which none can do for you. But I can weep with you and pray with you; and indeed I *am* doing both, for my tears blind me as I write, and I do not cease to pray for you. May you have all the help and light you need, and have it always. And, my dear, dear friend, Mr. J., too ('Millie's' father)—what a fearful trial for him!

* Lecturer on Botany at Westminster Hospital, Author of "Nature's Fairy-land," "Haunts of Nature," &c.

He has had much, very much to bear of bereavement and sorrow, and now this heart-breaking trouble to crown it all. I do hope he will know, and you too, my dearest H., that the ' Man of Sorrows ' is near you, and that your sorrow is so involved with His that He will certainly turn it into joy—for *her*, and for you, and for you all. Try to stay your soul with the faith of Christ—the faith He had in His Father, the faith He invites us to have in Himself. Our life is not rounded with death, but with a larger and fuller life. Last Sunday was the Resurrection Sunday. Our church was full of flowers, and I preached from, ' Thus it behoved Christ to suffer, and to rise from the dead the third day ' (Luke xxiv. 46). So it *did* behove Him, for He *was*, and *is*, and *will* be, and *must* be, ' life from the dead.'

"I shall see you, I hope, in the summer. But oh, my dear, dear boy, my journey will be sad. I go to two empty homes—my father's (my mother's, rather) and yours. God help us ! "

Did space permit, and could the veil that hides such sorrow be lifted, it would be seen that not once, but many times He bore His people's burdens and carried their griefs, as only a very deep and tender nature could do.

As I write I can think of one and another who will read these words and who will feel that *they* are included in what I say, though their names do not appear upon the printed page.

About seven years after his settlement in Reading the church building was enlarged and altered. During the renovation, Mr. Stevenson preached in the Town Hall to crowded congregations. At the reopening services Dr. Parker and Baldwin Brown were the preachers. Lunch was held in the school-room, where the ministers of the city and the special guests of the day were entertained by the Trinity congregation. It was a happy, and to the pastor a memorable occasion—one of those " white days" in the life of an earnest minister for which he can "thank God and take fresh courage." During the time when "the Disestablishment of the Irish Church " was agitating the nation, Mr. Stevenson was asked by the Liberal party to hold a meeting in the Town Hall and express their views on the question. This he did, and held a crowded audience for two hours. He was speaking on a subject full of interest to himself ; the sympathy of his audience roused him to his best, and at the close he was greeted with a perfect ovation.

Two or three times during his life in Reading he was visited by Thomas Cooper, once the celebrated Chartist leader, but in the days of which I speak a " Lecturer on Christianity " and veteran soldier of the cross.

As a lad, when visiting relations in Leicester, Mr. Stevenson had often watched, with awe-struck eyes, the army of starving men headed by their lusty champion, wearing a red cap of liberty, marching

through the Leicester market-place, and singing a
Chartist song, with the refrain—

> " The lion of freedom's released from his den,
>   We'll rally around him again and again."

And a leonine aspect even in those later years
Thomas Cooper presented. At that time, however,
" he roared as gently as a sucking dove," and
many delightful rambles did they have through
Reading and the surrounding country. Botany
was Mr. Cooper's favourite pastime, and he soon
had the young minister as fascinated as he was
himself in hunting after new " specimens," which
he enjoyed with all the freshness of a simple, un-
worldly nature. " Rich as a Devonshire lane," the
old gentleman pronounced the fields and hedges of
Berkshire, as they returned with their hands and
arms so full of treasures that their hostess was
fairly puzzled how to stow them away. To Thomas
Cooper he owed his fondness for botany, which ever
after made his country rambles so full of interest
to him. The writer has many happy recollections
of "a day's holiday " in the lovely valley of the
Thames, when wandering by the river-side in the
neighbourhood of Pangbourne or Maidenhead. A
zest was added to their enjoyment by the discovery
of some " bright particular " treasure among the
long meadow grasses or under the luxuriant
hedgerows.

And so the time sped on, unmarked by any

striking event, until pastor and people had been together for ten years. Mr. Stevenson now held a position possible only to one who had been so long "tried and proved." He had watched those who had been children on his arrival grow up into manhood and womanhood. He had buried those who had finished their course—had stood by their sickbeds, had become the loved and trusted counsellor in their times of perplexity. In the town itself he had grown to be an institution; and as one humourously remarked, "Reading without Mr. Stevenson would be as bad as 'Hamlet' without the Prince of Denmark." More than once efforts had been made to secure him for other churches, but he seemed proof against all temptations from without. A change, however, little contemplated on either hand, was in store for him.

In the winter of 1873, which proved a very damp and unhealthy one in Reading, bordering as it does on the valley of the Thames, Mr. Stevenson suffered much from neuralgia of the eyes. The trouble proving not only intensely painful, but persistent, his medical man wished him to consult a London oculist. This he did, and was advised to try prolonged rest, and if possible a sea voyage, as the best means of cure.

A trip to New York to attend the meetings of the Evangelical Alliance was therefore proposed in the following summer, and generously arranged for by his congregation. During his travels Mr.

Stevenson visited Montreal, and preached at the well-known Zion Congregational Church, for many years under the pastoral care of the venerable Dr. Wilkes, who has been called "the Father of Canadian Congregationalism." From the articles in the Montreal *Daily Witness* and other papers, it seems evident that Dr. Stevenson produced a marked impression during his visit, and the Zion Church congregation determined, if possible, to secure him. They were then under the pastorate of the Rev. C. Chapman, but the idea was to build a new church in the western portion of the city, at which fresh help would be required. Early in the following year, therefore, they forwarded Mr. Stevenson a hearty invitation, which was soon after enforced by the personal appeal of Dr. Wilkes himself, who visited England in that year, and laid the claims of the colony strongly before him.

For some time Mr. Stevenson underwent an anxious struggle of mind as to what it would be right to do. On the one hand were the close ties that bound him to his Reading charge; the fact also that both he and his wife would be called to part with beloved parents; his love for his native land, and his interest in her politics and general welfare. On the other hand there was the hope of improved health, the drier and more exhilarating Canadian climate having already benefited him, the future of his children, and the claims of Canadian Congregationalism. Decision proved a difficult task. Very earnestly did he and those who loved him seek for Divine guidance ; and we must believe that when at last he elected to serve the Church in Canada it was in obedience to the Master's call.

I must pass briefly over the time of painful excitement that followed, on his decision to leave England becoming publicly known. Farewell meetings, partings with old friends, public and private adieus, which tried him to the utmost, continued with little variation until he stood with wife and children on board the vessel which was to convey them to their Canadian home.

The first few months of Mr. Stevenson's new life were spent in adapting himself to his changed surroundings. Methods of work differed somewhat from those of the old country, and at first he felt the strangeness of his position. The winter was passed in Zion Church with Mr. (now Dr.) Chapman for his co-pastor, and then a separate church was formed, of which Mr. Stevenson was invited to take the sole charge, and the new building commenced in the western part of the city.

The editor of the Montreal *Witness*, himself a Congregationalist, says of Mr. Stevenson's work at this period : " The congregation grew. Many were attracted alike by his virile eloquence and his high philosophic cast of thought. He became a power not only in the church but in the city. . . . He had something for both mind and heart, and he

stirred the whole nature. He made truth inviting,
for in its delivery he charged the message with
something of his own warmth and colour and un-
faltering optimism."

A letter written by him about this time to the
Reading Church may be of interest here.

"To THE WORSHIPPERS AT TRINITY CONGREGATIONAL
CHURCH.

"MONTREAL, *February* 22, 1875.

"MY DEAR FRIENDS,—I am anxious to send you
a few words of greeting early in the year, and not
the less but the more because the wide Atlantic
rolls between us. I am very often amongst you in
imagination ; even as I write these lines I can see
the familiar faces, still very dear to me, amongst
whom they will probably be read. If only I had the
space-annihilating hat, the wearer of which could
be in an instant wherever he wished to be, how
soon would I come and spend a few hours in the
dear old church, or gather you all about me in the
schoolroom for a long and pleasant talk. Truly
there is much to be thankful for. If you have
half as pleasant thoughts of me as I have of you
(and I know you have), we shall have to be grateful
all our lives that we ever knew each other. My
life and work amongst you will be a pleasant
memory to me as long as I live.

"We are passing here through the cold of midwinter, and of a winter unusually severe even for Canada. For twenty-seven of the thirty-one days of January the thermometer was below zero, and sometimes as much as twenty-five and thirty degrees below. The ground has been covered with snow ever since the end of November, and will be till perhaps the end of March. The river St. Lawrence is frozen over so that we can drive heavy vehicles across it; the ice is not less than a foot thick. All wheeled carriages are put away and sleighs alone are seen in the streets or on the roads. They glide along in silence, so that we only know they are near by the tinkling of the bells on the horses. No description can give an idea of the beauty of the Canadian sky. It is of the purest and softest blue, and the sun shines as brightly as in summer. The sunlight is reflected brilliantly from the surface of the glittering snow. In spite of the cold, the winter is a most enjoyable season, and even against the cold we are well protected both by the systematic warming of our houses and by the appropriate clothing which we wear. We are all, I am thankful to say, in good health, and find our life in Canada very pleasant.

"My thoughts have turned to you very often with earnest desires that you may soon meet with a wise and good man who may take up and carry on the work of God amongst you as your pastor. I am reminded that some time must elapse before you can receive these lines, and it may be that in the interval my desire shall have been fulfilled. If so, I can only wish for my successor that he may find the unvarying kindness which was given to me, and that he may be far more successful in leading you to the loftier heights of the life which is hidden with Christ in God. If his ministry be in some respects different from mine, so much the better, for I am sure God has truth to teach you which it has not pleased Him to reveal to me. Try, my dear friends, to grow in the knowledge of Christ, and be ready to receive whatever light is shed, through whomsoever, upon His character and will. The whole purpose of life is to get near Him, to put on the new humanity which He has realized and waits to impart. Whatever helps us to do this is to be valued above our chief joy, and only what does not is to be regarded as spiritually irrelevant and untrue. What we chiefly need is a daily revelation of Christ to our souls, that we may be illumined in thought, emotion, and action by the light of His perfect mind. We may be thankful that the Divine Spirit is able and willing to use all sincere and devout ministry as a means to take of the things that are Christ's, and show them unto us.

" I thank those of you who have been so kind as to write to me or to Mrs. Stevenson since our arrival in Canada. Their letters, they may rest assured, have been most welcome, and have been read and read again with much affectionate thought of the writers. I must ask them to be kind enough not to feel hurt if they are not at once answered, for our time is much occupied, and it has often happened that, when we have intended to write, necessary duty has interposed a stern negative. Canada is a beautiful and happy country, but it is a very busy one; none need come hither who are afraid of work. But then the work is healthy, and happy, and productive, so that it is no penalty, but brings its own reward. I do not believe there is a country in the world where work done in the right spirit, and in the right way, is so rapidly followed by indications of success. Canadians are intelligent, quick-minded, and warm-hearted, and very appreciative of any one who honestly strives to be thorough and serviceable. I believe this is true in business life, and in the life of society generally, and I am sure it is true in the Church.

"Of course we have our difficulties. The chief of these is the prevalence of the Roman Catholic Church, at least in this province of Quebec, or, as it used to be called, Lower Canada. It is not exactly the Established Church—for we have no Established Church here—but it is the Church of the large majority. The French-speaking Canadians and those of Irish origin universally belong to it, and although there is little bitterness of feeling, or unseemly bigotry amongst us, yet in matters which concern religion we are too much separated. Of course it is not possible to win even

a hearing for Protestant ideas from a population
indoctrinated from childhood in the beliefs of
Rome; indeed I am afraid the very attempt to do
so, unless made with a rare degree of wisdom,
does more harm than good. But in no country,
on the other hand, are Protestants more united.
We work together, and live in mutual confidence
and affection. Our city is full of beautiful
churches, well attended, and the centre of a
vigorous religious life.

"Speaking of churches leads me to say that we
hope to build our new church as soon as the
weather will allow; or, at least, to begin the work.
I am very much encouraged by the energy and
enthusiasm with which the people gather round
me. I have no doubt that, with the blessing of
God, I shall have a useful and happy life here. My
health is good, and my prospects such as even my
partial and affectionate friends at Reading might
desire for me.

"If I do not send special messages of love, it is
that I have so much and for so many that I do not
know where to begin or end. May our Heavenly
Father bless you all, and keep you now and ever.

"Your ever affectionate friend,
　　　　　　　　　"J. F. STEVENSON."

The new church was completed in due time, and
christened "Emmanuel." From the beginning it
became endeared to its pastor, who had watched

its growth with much interest and anxiety; and
seemed likely to continue to be his as long as
he continued to preach. Again and again he
refused other calls without bringing them before
his people. It must not be supposed, however,
that he found Colonial life entirely a bed of roses.
Surrounded by men " making haste to be rich,"
finding keen competition not only in the world but
in the Church, it was often necessary to " endure
hardness," to " suffer loss," and to stand alone for
what he considered right and truth. Neither was
he altogether exempt from domestic trials. A few
months after his arrival, while as yet both he and
his wife were " strangers in a strange land," their
youngest child was taken from them after a three
days' illness. Her father had always made a
special pet of her, and I have the picture before
me now of the little creature mounted on his
shoulder, or carried to sleep in his arms. The
last day of her brief life she lay in the same
resting-place, and very hard he found it to give
her up. It is a consolation to believe that as her
little coffin rests upon her father's now, so in the
unseen world he has his child again, where their
freed and glorified spirits have entered a larger
and more blessed life.

A few years later came the death of his beloved
and venerated father. They had shared each
other's intellectual life for years, and when the
removal to Canada had taken place it was a

question which of the two felt the most gone out
of their lives. He longed to be able to comfort his
bereaved mother and sisters, and felt the three
thousand miles of ocean between them a hard
barrier at such a time.

If there were difficulties, however, there were
compensating advantages. The equality of the
religious denominations, now for the first time
experienced, was an unceasing delight to him. To
be one amongst other brother clergymen, after
having been simply "tolerated," was a most
refreshing change, and no one could have luxuri-
ated more in the sense of enlargement and freedom
which it gave him than Mr. Stevenson did. He felt
very strongly what he constantly affirmed "that
the variety of thought and opinion in different
sections of the Church was not a misfortune over
which to mourn but the natural expression and
necessary condition of a completely developed
life."

The absence of conventionality in Montreal
society, a certain frank and easy acceptance of
people and circumstances, had its charm for him,
while the brightness of the climate and the
exhilaration of the air were a much-needed
stimulus to him physically. In England he had
always been a sufferer from the cold, but the
effectual way in which Canadians heat their
houses, and the much drier quality of the air,
made the winter months as enjoyable in their own

way as the summer. No doubt the snow sometimes has its drawbacks, as, for instance, when a
whole train full of people are snowed up, and
obliged to wait till a snow-plough makes a cutting
for them. This happened to Mr. Stevenson on one
or two occasions—rather amusingly once, when
Montreal papers spoke of the "able and eloquent
speech" which he had delivered at Quebec, thereby
setting at rest the anxieties of his wife, who had
feared to see him set out in so severe a storm;
the fact of the case being that, while the papers
announced him as speaking in Quebec, he and his
companions were sitting in "durance vile," snowed
up between the two cities. But here again they
had the advantage of well-warmed cars, and the
possibility of obtaining refreshments, which would
not have been the case in England. He was a
great lover of the beauty of nature; and the
picturesqueness of Montreal—the broad blue of
the St. Lawrence, and the varying loveliness of
the mountain, especially when autumn hangs out
her golden and rosy banners amongst the maples,
were a never-ceasing delight to him.

During his eleven years in Canada he made
some valuable friendships. Amongst these must
be mentioned the name of the Rev. Dr. Norman,
now Dean of the English Cathedral in Quebec, at
that time resident in Montreal. With him he
worked in the cause of education with much
sympathy; and when Mr. Stevenson, owing to

4

overwork, resigned the chairmanship of the Protestant School Board, Dr. Norman succeeded to the vacant post. A letter from him, published with other reminiscences later in this volume, will show how much they were one in thought and feeling. With the Very Rev. Dr. Grant, Principal of Queen's University, Kingston, Ontario, he formed a friendship severed only by death. From this University, at the hands of the Principal, Dr. Stevenson received his D.D. degree. He had obtained his LL.B. several years previously at his own London University.

His hold upon the young was very strong. He often called them "the joy and crown" of his ministry. On their part they were not slow to understand and appreciate a man so much in touch with their interests. Since his death I have had many letters from young men full of grief for his loss, and all testifying to his usefulness and helpfulness to them. He was particularly happy when addressing the students, whether of his own Theological College or of the University. I have before me a note written by Sir William Dawson, Principal of McGill University, after Dr. Stevenson had spoken at the annual dinner of the undergraduates.

"McGill College,
"*Dec.* 19, 1882.

"My dear Dr. Stevenson,—Permit me to follow an impulse which seizes me this morning, in

thanking you for the very excellent speech with
which you favoured us last evening. I have seldom
heard anything better suited to the undergraduate
mind, or more likely to do good and fructify
therein ; and I am sure you will admit that this
is what it is meant to be—very high commendation.

" Again thanking you, I remain,

" Yours truly,

" J. W. Dawson."

In 1882 the Congregational College was erected
in Montreal, and Dr. Stevenson was urged to become
the Principal. Most of his own leading people
were members of the College Board of Directors,
and felt the necessity of obtaining as Principal a
man of culture and influence, who yet should not
be wholly dependent upon the College for support.
The doctor's first impressions were that it would
be impossible to add to his already busy life so
important a charge as the College must prove.
Upon the deacons, however, undertaking to relieve
him as far as possible of pastoral visitation, and
promising all the aid in their power in the work of
the church, he at length consented. His new work
proved highly congenial to him. Principal and
students mutually attracted each other. His house
opened into the College, and it was seldom that
some " young brother " was not to be found in
the doctor's study. His talks with the students,
whether collectively or individually, were full of

interest to him; and they on their part never abused the privileges he granted them, but felt for him all the loyal and enthusiastic regard so natural to the young.

Congenial as the work was, however, it was too much when added to his position as pastor of an important church. His health, which had seemed much improved during his earlier years in Canada, began to show signs of failure. He was, in fact, doing the work of two men. He did not know the art, either, of husbanding what strength he had. Into everything he did he put the whole of himself, disregarding the consequent exhaustion. After carrying on his double work for three years it became evident to those who loved him best that he was doing more than he could stand. The vacation, and a trip to England, it was hoped, would re-establish health again. He had rather unusual recuperative power, and it was somewhat remarkable that, delicate as he was, he had hardly ever been prevented from preaching by illness during the whole of his ministry.

While in London on this occasion he preached for two Sundays in the now vacant pulpit of his late beloved and honoured friend, the Rev. James Baldwin Brown. Dr. Stevenson was no stranger to the Brixton Church; he had repeatedly preached there during Baldwin Brown's ministry. He did not, however, regard himself as a candidate for the pulpit, as at the time another name was before its members which it seemed most probable would be accepted. Circumstances arising, not necessary to be detailed here, which left the pastorate still open, the congregation, many of whom were personal friends of the doctor's, turned to him very naturally as the man of their choice.

Once again, therefore, the anxious question of a change of pastorates had to be faced; and the difficulty of arriving at a decision was no less great than on the former occasion. It will not be thought surprising that Dr. Stevenson left England without giving any decided answer to the invitation of the Brixton Church. His Canadian, like his Reading pastorate, had been of more than ten years' duration. Both his elder sons had settled in Montreal, and his ties to the New World seemed as strong as those to the old. When asked afterwards by an English friend what had decided him to make the change, he replied, " The desire to be near my dear old mother in her declining years, and the honour of standing in Baldwin Brown's pulpit."

He had never anticipated the burst of feeling on the part not only of his own people, but of Montreal generally, when his intention to leave them became known. To his astonishment he found that " the whole city was moved," Catholics and Protestants uniting in a farewell banquet to testify their regard to one who had become as " a Canadian to the Canadians" during his residence amongst them.

Too many Englishmen in their travels behave as
though they could teach all and learn nothing, as
one of the speakers on the occasion remarked. Dr.
Stevenson, by his modesty and sympathy, had
made himself a power in the community, and the
loss they were to sustain they felt would prove a
heavy one.

On the first Sunday of December, 1886, Dr.
Stevenson occupied the Brixton pulpit for the first
time as its pastor. His text was, "God hath been
mindful of us, He will bless us," from the 115th
Psalm and 12th verse. It was a fit introduction to
his brief, bright ministry among them—a ministry
which to be permitted to undertake he felt to be the
crowning honour of his life. At his recognition
service the chair was occupied by his old friend
Dr. Hannay, and among others who were met to
give him welcome was the gifted and beloved Dr.
Elmslie, with whom he afterwards enjoyed an
intimate acquaintance. Now they have all three
finished their earthly work, and entered into nobler
service above. May God raise up faithful men to
take their places, and especially may the new
pastor at Brixton prove a true successor in spirit
and life to those who have gone before.

And now once more back in his beloved South
London, close to the haunts of his youthful days,
amongst a people already in large measure endeared, the lines seemed to have fallen for him

in pleasant places. His walks were often rambles amid old surroundings. Early friends were constantly meeting him; and almost every Sunday some one would come into his vestry who, as one of them said, "must shake hands with the doctor, as they had known him when he was a little fellow in pinafores." Many old Canadian friends, too, who were frequently in the Metropolis, would find their way to the Brixton Church, feeling, as they looked at his happy and prosperous surroundings, more reconciled to his having left them. In the midst of so large a church he had neither the time nor the opportunity for so much outside work as he had formerly undertaken, but his interest in the cause of progress and education was as keen as ever. One not personally known to him writes in a current number of a magazine : "The writer well remembers hearing him speak in Exeter Hall, in the company of some bishops and churchmen, upon 'Christian Evidences.' He made a splendid speech, and a friend near remarked, 'The best speech to-day ; the man has a future.' That future has indeed been sadly cut short."

To use words of Dr. Stevenson's quoted from a speech made to his congregation on the occasion of his silver wedding, which they had most generously memorialized, will serve to show the happy relation between pastor and people: "Nearly two years ago I came to be with you. When first coming among you I was welcomed as a man could scarcely ex-

pect to be. You have taken me into your hearts by
your kindness; I have taken you into mine; and
I desire no greater privilege in this world than to
be a successful minister, if it be God's will, of the
congregation I now serve, and the church I love so
well. And when, in God's time, it becomes my
duty to lay down the charge which you have en-
trusted to me, then may He grant that the grand
work done by my predecessor, and the work, by
His mercy, that I am endeavouring to do in succes-
sion to him, may be taken up by some able man
and carried forward into the indefinite future with
still greater and wider blessing."

Alas! those who heard him little thought how
very short his time was, and how soon " the church
he loved so well " would have to mourn his loss.
On his first returning to England Dr. Stevenson's
health had seemed much benefited by the change.
The doctors spoke hopefully of his condition, and
he himself inclined to the belief that as he grew
older he would probably become more robust than
he ever was as a young man. No doubt his London
life caused him a certain amount of excitement;
and though his work deeply interested him, yet it
" took it out of him," as he himself used to say,
pretty severely.

Perhaps one of the, to him, most interesting
public events that took place during his residence in England was the opening of Mansfield
College, Oxford. He was a guest, on the occasion,

of Professor Edward Poulton, whose knowledge of natural science is giving him a high reputation in Oxford, and in whom the doctor was greatly interested, Mr. Poulton having been one of his " Reading boys." Dr. Stevenson's own account of the opening may be recorded here, as best showing how he was affected by the new movement. It was sent to one of the periodicals, at the time, and entitled " At Oxford."

" There he stood, with white, venerable hair, the first of English Greek scholars, with Blackie, first of Scottish scholars in the same mighty language, not far from him. And what did he say, he, Dr. Jowett, who has unsphered the spirit of Plato for all men ? ' This,' said he, ' is a great day of reconciliation. Let us forgive and forget the past.' He did not say, ' Let us forget our principles,' or, ' Let us be false to the heroisms of our respective histories '; he was too wise and too noble for that. But he saw, and made us see, that out of the strifes of bygone years, strifes which have made uniformity impossible, there might arise a finer and a grander unity than even the wisest of our fathers dreamed. He spoke of all schemes of ' Comprehension ' as inept and futile, while he pleaded for a mutual understanding which should issue in a mutual respect. And he saw in what we were doing then—claiming and taking a place in the life of the old University around which cluster the associations of a thousand

years of English culture—the augury of a future
which would gather up the benefits of past pain
and sorrow, and realize 'the far-off interest of
tears.'

"He was not alone. The ripest learning, the
profoundest thought, the most brilliant research of
the University were gathered around him. There
sat men whose work, in literature, in theology,
in natural and anthropological science, has made
their names household words with all the more
studious amongst us. It is not too much to say
that the very pith and marrow of what is most
characteristic and most brilliant in the life of
Oxford was represented there. The men who are
forming the future of our national thought and
character were conspicuous by their presence and
manifest sympathy. The sense that a certain
epoch was closing, and another of a different
character was beginning to open upon us was what
imparted the peculiar quality to our thought and
emotion. The older epoch had been one of narrow
sympathies and partial views; the new was to involve completer insight into the subjects of research
and a larger respect for fellow-workers.

"One element in the sense of a coming unity
was the consciousness of a truer and more fruitful
method of study. 'Systems,' we felt, had been
on all sides too complete to be true. They were
giving way. Science, with its inductive investigation, its cautious verification, its sense of the

infinity of truth, and its profound humility, was taking the place of systems. When the spirit of reverent inquiry and of love for fact is beating in all hearts, the boundary lines which divide various ' schools' grow gradually more faint and dim. The wealth and power of facts, in whatever department of inquiry, philology, interpretation, anthropology, history of events, or of doctrines, constitute an inheritance open to us all ; and men of all sections of the Church have already done, and are still doing, so much good work that it is impossible to look on each other as any longer really divided. What is the chaff to the wheat ? What are outward modes of organization or worship to the stores of knowledge surely accumulating, and the spirit of devout fervour common to all earnest men ? Opinions may tend to separation ; the study of facts and of the principles they disclose must draw towards unity.

"I think we felt, too, on all sides, the profound truth of Bacon's saying, 'They be two things— Unity and Uniformity.' The Church is not a regiment of soldiers, each clothed and armed exactly like the others. It is a living body, every member different from the rest, but together forming a majestic and glorious unity. As the trunk, the boughs, the leaves, the flowers, the fruit of a magnificent tree are the embodiment and expression of a common energy, and as no part has any true being except in relation to the rest, so the variety of the Church is not a misfortune over which to mourn, but the necessary condition of a completely developed life. Perhaps no member, however small or obscure, is without its significance. To the eye of God, it may be, every mode of Christian thought and worship adds something to the ideal completeness, and even seeming discords enhance the complicated harmony.

"We represented the 'National Church.' Yet the National Church is not bounded by the 'State' Church; she includes us all. Now that our ministry are to be trained in closer neighbourhood; now that we are drinking in the spirit of the same sacred culture; now that the associations, at once holy and romantic, of the queen of academical cities are again our common possession, we may hear in thought the holy bells that ring out old prejudices and meaningless antagonisms, and ring in the complete and reconciling reign of 'the Christ that is to be.'

"Better omens for these hopes we could not have. The college is noble and beautiful, its teachers learned, godly, and wise. The spirit in which it is welcomed is generous and kindly in the highest degree. It needs only work, faith, and prayer, and the fresh morning that now dawns on the ministry of our churches will shine brighter and brighter unto the perfect day."

An extract from a letter to his mother will show how engagements kept him occupied.

"My Dearest Mother,—We are in the thick of the May meetings, and a very dense 'thick' it is. I am already very tired, and feel as though the best thing I could do would be to go to bed, and, if possible, to sleep for the next twenty-four hours. But, alas! I have been to the missionary sermon with M. this morning to hear Hugh Price Hughes (who preached admirably), and must, when I have finished this, go and dress for dinner, to meet Dr. Bruce and other guests, at the house of a good friend of ours, Mr. Peter Mason. Yesterday we had the morning session of the Union at the City Temple, after which about a dozen of the most venerable of us—Drs. Allon, Dale, Hannay, Rogers, Falding, and others—all white-headed—dined with Dr. Parker. I went straight from the dinner to the Memorial Hall to tea, and thence to the City Temple, where we had a splendid meeting of the Church Aid Society. Two village ministers made admirable speeches, and I spoke my best to conclude. We held a very fine audience to the close; so you will see our meetings go excellently. . . . J. and E. Goadby called on me a week ago, and we had a long talk about poor Tom.* His death upset me so much that for some days I was really ill. . . . We are doing excellently well at the church; the congregations fuller than ever before, and the people full of kindness. . . . By

* Rev. Thomas Goadby, B.A., Principal of the Baptist College, Nottingham.

the way, the other day I met Dr. Fitch at the Brixton Training School. I was a monitor at the Borough Road School when he saw me *last;* yet he recognized me in an instant—over a space of fully forty years ! "

In the autumn of 1889, the doctor seeming somewhat worn with the year's work, his people gave him an extended holiday, in which it was hoped that a thorough rest might re-invigorate him. They made the stipulation that no work was to be done during the vacation, an agreement he faithfully carried out, and spent most of his time in Switzerland, which he greatly enjoyed, and which seemed at the time of much benefit to him.

Writing from Lucerne, he says :—

"I think the extra time has been useful; I am sure it has been enjoyable. You can form no idea of the beauty of this lake and these mountains, in the perfect weather of Wednesday and to-day. I do not know whether day, or evening, or starlight is the more lovely. There is not a cloud in the sky—only a faint, delicate haze which softens the outline of the hills and idealizes the whole prospect. The temperature, though warm, is delightful. We have a very interesting party here." And so on. A friend remarked that wherever *he* was there was always sure to be an interesting party. He had the happy faculty of drawing out the best in every one.

No subject of conversation was started to which he could not add something worth hearing, and all his resources were placed at the disposal of those who so demanded them. Switzerland, from first to last, was one long delight to him, and he returned home refreshed in body and mind. The winter was one of unceasing engagements, and more or less exciting work, but it did not seem to tax his strength unduly. In February he began a series of special Sunday evening sermons on the "Essentials of Religion." The course was as follows :—" Belief in God"; " Character of God"; " Future Life—its possibility"; " Future Life—our right to it"; " Future Life—its necessity"; " Retribution — its equity"; " Retribution — its mercy"; " The Good News."

It is the writer's very great regret that these sermons cannot be reproduced. On all hands he was urged to publish them; and even when it became evident that his public work was ended, he hoped to have strength enough to revise the rough notes and crude reports, so that they might be made ready for the press. He had spent much time and thought in his pulpit preparation for them, and probably, after a hard winter's work, the exhaustion consequent upon this, and the excitement of delivering them in the heat of a crowded audience, served to hasten the end.

After preaching the last sermon of the course, he went home greatly fagged, and said to his wife,

" Have I talked sense to-night ? I feel strangely beclouded, and cannot tell now a word I said." During the week he went with his wife to the sea-side, and seemed somewhat brighter ; returning for the following (Easter) Sunday services. The day passed much as usual, and those who listened to him had little idea that they heard his voice for the last time. Had they known it some of his words would have sounded strangely significant, and the Easter lilies with which loving hands had adorned the pulpit, might have seemed as " a preparation beforehand for his burial." The text of the evening was, " Who shall change the body of our humiliation, and fashion it like unto His glorious body." All of it that was written appears at the close of this volume. Unfortunately it is impossible to reproduce the happy inspiration which he used to say was "given him at the moment," and which, when he at all enjoyed preaching, added to his sermons what the aroma gives to the flower—a something which can never be recalled.

The next day, accompanied by his wife, he set out for Ventnor, hoping that rest would again do for him what it had so often done before. But actual disease had set in, and every day increased his restlessness and misery. After a week of suffering days and sleepless nights he wrote to his deacons that he felt he must resign his charge. Amazed and perplexed, unable to believe in the rapid development of his illness, the deacons urged his trying a longer rest, generously promising that his pulpit should be kept open for him as long as there was a chance of his recovery. It seemed only wise to try what time would do, and from Ventnor he went to Matlock, thinking that perhaps mountain air might be more beneficial to him than the sea. But time and place made no difference, " the iron band around his head " (as he described the constant pain he felt) only tightened its cruel clasp, and Matlock did no more for him than Ventnor.

The physicians united in pronouncing it brain disease, the one and only chance of recovery being immediate cessation of work, and entire rest of body and mind. There was nothing before him, therefore, than to resign his beloved charge immediately; and the stroke fell heavily indeed upon pastor and people alike. A member of the congregation, going into the church one morning during that sad week, saw the doctor standing in front of the pulpit with tears running down his cheeks. He had taken farewell of his church and his work for ever. So " he entered into the cloud "—a cloud which slowly deepened around him until the end.

The physicians he consulted thought it possible that a change to Canada and the companionship of his two elder sons might be of some benefit to him. The voyage was accordingly undertaken;

and in August, 1890, Dr. Stevenson, with his wife and two younger children, returned to Montreal. It was a sad return! Three years and nine months before he had left Canada, full of hope for the future; he came back a weary, worn, and broken man, to look once more into his sons' faces before he died. Old friends gathered around him full of tenderness and sympathy. Homes where many happy days had been spent were opened to him, and love came with hands full of offerings to help and comfort; but in vain. It was impossible that any change should bring permanent relief. A gleam of his old brightness shone out now and again, and hope would momentarily revive, only to be quenched in still deeper darkness. Autumn waned into winter, but no relief came to the aching head and throbbing nerves. Christmas Day he was able to spend with his family, and for awhile the expiring lamp of mental light shot up a few bright rays. It was the last effort, and the last memory given to wife and children of the dear familiar form which joined the fireside circle for the last time that evening. A terrible relapse followed; and for the next month he suffered as few are called to suffer. Day and night were alike a " dimness of anguish," all that makes life worth living having been shut out from his existence. Thus he lingered until the 1st of February, 1891. But the Heavenly Father had not forgotten His suffering son, and the cup of sorrow was well-nigh drained. " Very early in the morning on the first day of the week," came the summons of release. The immediate cause of his death was heart-failure; and he passed quietly away in his sleep, with no apparent pain or struggle, from the darkness and the mystery which had beset him for a little while, into the never-ending " joy of his Lord."

The funeral service was held in the church that had been built for him—Emmanuel Church. The students of the college of which he had been Principal attended in a body, and laid an anchor of white flowers among the many wreaths upon his coffin. The church was filled with mourners, including all the principal men of the city, whose presence there was something more than a mere formality. The service was conducted by the Rev. W. H. Pulsford, the newly-elected pastor of the church, and the Rev. Dr. Barbour, now Principal of the college. Prayer, especially for the widow and children, was offered very tenderly by the Rev. Dr. Cornish; and two of Dr. Stevenson's favourite hymns, " Our God, our help in ages past," and " Lead, kindly light," were sung. The Rev. James Barclay, minister of St. Paul's Presbyterian Church, then gave the following address :—

" We are met here to mourn the death of one

who was greatly respected and much beloved in this community, and who but very recently was worthily honoured by it for the life he had lived and the work he had done in it—a life and work commending themselves to all men in the sight of God. From many a sorrowing heart we can fancy the question rising, ' Can it be that that fine intellect, so beautifully cultured and so greatly enriched, and that gentle, generous heart, so full of such deep and tender sympathies, are extinguished for ever?' It cannot be; such is not our faith. The world is richer and better to-day because he lived; and for himself, what was begun here shall be perfected hereafter. Dr. Stevenson was a man who read much, thought much, and felt deeply, and, owing to his strong sympathies, suffered not a little. He was a man who loved warmly and was loved by many, a man whose life from its inherent beauty, apart altogether from the great gifts with which he was endowed, could not but be an influence for good wherever he moved. There was a great charm in his conversation, flowing as it did from an unusually richly stored and appreciative mind and singularly suggestive memory, and from a broad, generous heart. Few who had the privilege of hearing him will easily forget his public utterances from pulpit and platform. Whatever the theme he handled, his audience at once felt themselves raised above all pettiness to a high level of thought and feeling; to listen to him was to have one's better nature stirred, to be made to think and feel that life was a high and holy thing. His thoughts were impressive, the result of extensive reading, careful study, rich culture, and profound personal conviction, while the words in which he clothed them were musically eloquent, and the courteous and reverent earnestness of his manner constrained respectful attention and, with most, sympathetic affection. He was a man of keen sensitiveness—a sensitiveness which, if it sometimes caused him suffering, yet gave him force, for it winged the arrows of his arguments and gave point, poetry, and pathos to his thoughts. But it was this that aged him before his time, and though but a few years ago he bravely and vigorously took up the plough in a new field, bringing matured experience to the work, it was apparent to those who knew him best that his working day was not to be a long one. The intensity with which he threw himself into anything he did soon told its tale, and at a comparatively early age he had to retire from active service, conscious, however, as he must have been, that the 'well done, good and faithful servant' was stamped by the Master on his life-work, and in his enforced retirement he had the sweet solace and satisfaction of knowing that his life and work had not been in vain. It was given to him to know something of the affectionate regard he had won, of the kindly things that were thought and said of him, of the

help, and light, and strength, and peace he had
been the means of bringing into other hearts and
lives. Many of us, who knew him as a brother-
worker, remember with thankfulness and miss
with regret his broad-minded charity—that spirit
which had no sympathy with anything narrow-
minded or small—that spirit which, while loyal to
the special branch of the Church to which he belonged, thought far more and breathed far more of
the Church Catholic—that spirit which made as
little as possible of the differences that divide us,
and as much as possible of the sweet and sacred
ties that link us to one another. He believed in
the brotherhood of men, and he· lived his faith,
affording ground, beautiful ground, where others
who differed from him (differed widely in some ways)
could gladly meet him. He was a lover of truth
far more than of tradition—of truth for its own
sake, and truth from every quarter. He recognized
and claimed as an inalienable privilege every
man's right to think for himself. Very early in
my ministry in Montreal I received a kindly,
helpful, truly brotherly note from him, in which,
among other things, he wrote : 'Some of us in our
younger days suffered for liberty, suffered in influence and reputation, but it is an ample reward
to see a race of clergymen not more than ten or
twelve years younger than we preaching with power
and acceptance the principles which are dear to our
hearts.' We may say of him what was lovingly

said of another, 'A purer aspiration for truth, a
readier devotion to all clear right, a simpler trust
in a Divine light and life hid within every cloud
can rarely be found in a human soul.' He has
passed through the cloud a little before us, and
reached, I surely think, that light and life; and
that his sufferings are thus transformed may well
lend a little brightness to such duties, whether of
action or of patience, as may remain to those who
cannot cease to think of him. He has left a light
which not only reflects past worth, but shines yet
in blessing on his home and fellow-men. His loving
voice will fall no more upon our ear, but it is not
silent; though dead he yet speaks, and speaks
with a power which has a new sacredness in it.
His character will be remembered and his words
will be quoted and treasured by many, by some
who, perhaps, feel that during his life they yielded
themselves too little to the sweet and holy influence of his teaching. He will be remembered
by many in this congregation as one who made
truth clearer, goodness easier, duty more commanding; by many as one who strengthened their
faith, brightened their hopes, and gave life to
their best purposes. To all such he yet speaketh,
and to those who knew him best and loved him
most, his gentle voice will still speak sweetly,
lovingly, from the other side of that land of which
he thought so much, and of the realities of which
he had so firm a hold. They remember with

profound thankfulness what he was in life; they
treasure as a precious inheritance his beautiful
character, his powerful intellect, linked, as we
rarely see it, with a gentle heart; the words he
spoke, the kindnesses he rendered, the charity he
not only spoke but lived.

> " 'And though his tongue be silent,
>   Though empty now his place,
>   Though ne'er again his fellow-men
>   Will meet him face to face,
>
> " ' Yet still some wingèd mission
>   May catch the listening air,
>   And to the hearts that love him
>   Some thought of feeling bear.'

" Whilst we sorrow for the widow and family in
their present affliction, we rejoice that through
their tears they look back with gratitude to God
to a life so useful, so honoured, so beautiful, so
loving.   It is an heirloom which any family may
well treasure, and with calm confidence we think
of him now,

> " ' In His arms enfolded,
>   At His feet laid down,
>   Anchored in the shadow
>   Of the Eternal throne.' "

Before leaving the church, while the strains of
Handel's " Dead March " sounded from the organ,
the congregation passed slowly in front of the
coffin, so that all might look once more upon the

face of him who had been the pastor of many, and the friend of all—the face upon which, as they saw, had settled a heavenly peace. Then they bore him through the drifting snow to his resting-place in the beautiful cemetery of Mount Royal; and on the following Sunday a memorial service was held in Emmanuel Church, conducted by the Rev. Dr. Wells, pastor of the American Presbyterian Church.

EXTRACTS FROM THE MEMORIAL SERMON PREACHED BY THE REV. DR. WELLS IN EMMANUEL CHURCH, FEBRUARY 8, 1891.

" Now we see through a glass darkly ; but then face to face: now I know in part; but then shall I know even as also I am known."—1 COR. xiii. 12.

. . . I have chosen this thought in loving memory of our dear friend whose recent death we mourn. I believe it is the view of heaven which he liked best to take, in which he found the greatest cheer and joy, and which is also best adapted to console our hearts and to reconcile us to his loss. Is it not pleasant and comforting to think of him as safely passed beyond the pain and weakness of this mortal strife, and coming to the goodly fellowship and the glad activities of heaven ?

How will his sensitive, responsive spirit expand

and glow in that society—he who had so rare a gift and genius for companionship as to render him the choicest fellow and the truest friend?

Yet he was like a tender plant, and he keenly felt the slightest evil or unfriendly breath.

Now, for the first time, he meets only those who are most worthy and congenial to himself. I can almost see him as he seeks out one and another whom he knew, and who have gone before him home; yet not alone the friends whose faces he had seen, but that still greater throng with whom he was acquainted through their writings and their works—the earnest, restless thinkers to whom he was so near allied: the poets whose lines he loved so much and could so well repeat; especially the great hymn writers, whose holy songs he used to read so sweetly that the interpreter seemed scarcely less inspired than the author. How musical and rhythmical his voice became in such reading, and how entirely he was possessed and swayed by the spirit of the hymn! A few of us were once talking together of our favourite hymns. For a little while he was silent, while one or another quoted those we liked. While he listened the fire burned. Presently he broke forth, first with Charles Wesley's,

> " For ever here my rest shall be
> Close to Thy bleeding side,
> This all my hope and all my plea —
> For me the Saviour died."

Then came Watts's matchless version of the 90th
Psalm :—

> " Our God, our help in ages past,
>   Our hope for years to come,
>   Our refuge from the stormy blast,
>   And our eternal home."

The stream of sacred song flowed on, accompanied by his appreciative and kindly words. The
rest were glad to pause and listen.

> " Come, oh, Thou Traveller unknown,
>   Whom still I hold but cannot see,"

followed, and in all the years of our acquaintance
I never heard him speak more delightfully or
feelingly than then.*

What catholic and loving intercourse does he
now hold with those from every branch and
portion of the Christian Church, and some who
were of no church ; for, like Dr. Bushnell, he
believed in " outside saints," and held with Peter,
" that God is no respecter of persons, but in every

---

* Charles Wesley's hymns were almost his manual of devotion ; he could always enjoy a service in which they formed
a part. Writing from a country place he says : " I went this
morning to the Primitive Methodist Church, where we had
four of Charles Wesley's hymns, and one of Watts's, " Sweet
fields beyond the swelling flood," &c. A simple sermon,
defective in grammar, but filled with the Spirit. It was a
" blessed season."

nation he that feareth Him and worketh righteousness is accepted of Him."

It seemed a strange, but it was a very kind Providence which led Dr. Stevenson, a few years since, again to England, and permitted him to spend his latest years and do his closing work in the old home.

He was a man of the widest and quickest sympathies, ready to see and welcome the good qualities of every race and clime. He was fond of Canada, and found great pleasure in the freedom of this new land from some of the restraints and customs that still linger in the old. But, after all, he was first and always an Englishman—without the narrow prejudice and pride that mark some Englishmen—but with a world of patriotism and tenderness for country in his heart. Upon the whole I think he missed more than he found in Canada. He never felt entirely at home and at rest with us, though he would not own it. I believe he always was a little homesick for the mother-land. I have heard his voice tremble and seen his eyes glisten and moisten while speaking of it in a way that proved to me his heart still lingered there. London especially he loved as ardently as Lamb, or Thackeray, or Dickens did.

So when he was cordially invited back to England and London, and asked to be pastor of the very charge which he had sometimes said he would prefer above all others, we were far more sorry than surprised that he should go.

There he literally stood upon his native heath. He had spent his boyhood in the next parish, Camberwell, and must have often roamed and played around the spot on which his church was built.

He returned to his youthful home in the full zenith of reputation and of power. He plunged at once, with a zeal sharpened by years of absence, into the full tide and whirl of the great metropolis. He strongly felt the stir and stimulus of all its social, moral, and intellectual movement. Some of us doubted if it were well and wise for him to venture back, as his health had already showed some signs of giving way. But none of us who saw him and knew the eager interest and joy with which he lived and laboured there, can ever feel regret because he went. It was the fitting gracious crown that God in mercy placed upon his work. Whether the excitement and enjoyment of that closing period shortened his life and hastened its end at all we cannot tell. But even if it did, we will be glad that he should spend it in his chosen place and task.

He was able to preach for the last time on Easter Sunday of last spring. In the evening his text was in the words of St. Paul—Phil. iii. 21 —that read in the New Version which he used: " Who shall fashion anew the body of our humiliation, that it may be conformed to the body of His glory, according to the working whereby He is able even to subject all things unto Himself." The subject was well suited to his taste, and his mind, which had at times been weakened, broke forth in all its natural brilliancy and eloquence, and he preached a sermon unusual in its sweetness and strength.

> " Servant of God, well done !
> Rest from thy loved employ ;
> The battle fought, the victory won,
> Enter thy Master's joy."

He has now entered a greater and more goodly city, he has been admitted to a more elect and choice society—even "the general assembly and church of the firstborn, whose names are written in heaven."

Better and more precious than even the companionship of heaven will be for Dr. Stevenson its vigour and its opportunities for thought and work. His was an active and inquiring mind. He knew not how to rest. I never met him that I did not find him revolving some great question, enjoying some new work, exulting in some fresh treasure of wisdom or of beauty he had found. It was his heaviest cross that the mind could not do all that he wished it to perform. Sometimes after long reasoning upon a subject he would say : "Ah, well, I cannot find my way through it now, but it is good to think I shall know sometime." That blessedness is given to him now. He has not fathomed all the depths nor surmounted all the heights as yet, but he is thinking, searching, discovering, pressing on. The brain that grew so tired and ached so sorely here, is no more bound nor pained. The spirit was willing, but the flesh was weak. Now the body of humiliation is transformed into a glorious body, and has become the able and unwearied servant of the soul.

Let us lift up our eyes, dear friends, and look at him to-day, enjoying the blessed communion of the saints in light, engaged in blissful occupations of the redeemed who stand about the throne and who roam the boundless fields of heaven. Surely we will not wish him back. Rather will we rejoice that he is gone where he shall " see as he is seen, and know as he is known."

With humble, grateful hearts we bow our heads and say: "The Lord gave, and the Lord hath taken away ; blessed be the name of the Lord."

EXTRACT FROM A MEMORIAL SERMON PREACHED BY REV. J. JACKSON GOADBY, OF HENLEY-ON-THAMES, IN TRINITY CONGREGATIONAL CHURCH, READING.

"And Enoch walked with God; and he was not, for God took him."—GEN. v. 24.

. . . What better, what fitter words could one select to describe the character of your friend and mine than these words which tell us of the character of Enoch? The only qualification I have to speak of John Frederick Stevenson is this—a life-long acquaintance and intimacy. I knew him in the heyday of his youth, when hope was bright and heart was strong. I knew him in his riper manhood, and in his later years. I was with him in a time of sorrow, the bitterest that ever wrung and rent the human heart. I have been with him in seasons of joy and gladness. I knew him as few knew him, knew him in the sacred privacy of the closest and most intimate friendship, a friendship that was interrupted, but that was never for one moment broken. And I have no hesitation in saying, from this knowledge of him, that the dominant fact of his life was this—" He walked with God." To him God was the living God, ever near, ever present, ever loving, his Father and his Friend; and with a strong and tenacious grasp he held fast the hand of God stretched out to him in Jesus Christ.

Probably you know, as well as I know, the simple facts of his life : that his father and grandfather were both Nonconformist ministers of note, and did excellent work in their day, and that our friend was born in 1833. At sixteen years of age he began a course of study at the London University. The following year he entered as a student the college now known as Regent's Park College, but then situated in Stepney. In his twenty-first year he took his B.A. degree at the London University, and soon after became the minister of a Nonconformist church in Long Sutton, Lincolnshire. From thence he removed to Mansfield Road Chapel, Nottingham, as co-pastor of Rev. A. Syme, M.A., and on Mr. Syme's resignation he became the sole pastor. From Nottingham he came to be your minister in 1863. What he was to you while he was with you is best known to yourselves ; but this is certainly true—that since his removal in 1874 no other Nonconformist minister has ever occupied the same position of general influence in this town. What he has been elsewhere, in Montreal, and in London, it will hardly be possible for me to say.

A student from his earliest years, his mind was ever eager, active, and inquiring. He delighted to seize on principles, and to illustrate them. Philosophic and scientific studies always had for him an especial fascination. With a keen love of the best English literature, prose and verse, he had a fastidious taste, that made him reluctant to appear in print.   He possessed, in an eminent degree, the power of abstraction, and could at once, if he wished, pin himself down to any subject. Always a conscientious worker, he knew and respected honest work in others.

As a preacher you surely know better what he was than I. That he loved his work, that he thought it the noblest in which any man could engage, that he was a prophet rather than a priest, and that he was careful and conscientious in his pulpit preparation, is entirely true. But he did not neglect self-preparation while seeking to give of his best to others. He firmly believed that God's good news was far too broad to be narrowed down into a party Shibboleth, that it concerned all men everywhere, and that it was a message for all time. Whilst rising quickly to new ideas, he did not at once reject the old, but only after long and careful deliberation. A close student of God's Word, he sought the best human helps he could obtain for its interpretation, and also asked fervently for the aid of the Divine Spirit. He had these qualifications for a faithful and attractive preacher—an impassioned eloquence, a quick sympathy with men in all the phases of human experience, a reverent spirit, and an ardent desire to benefit his hearers. His prayers in the public services were the very pleadings of a man who felt in the presence of God, and made you feel it, and often left lasting impressions on the heart. He had not a few of the necessary gifts of a successful speaker. His voice was clear and penetrating, and yet sympathetic in quality. It could melt by its pathetic tones, or arouse by its enthusiasm. He rarely spoke, when at his best, without kindling with his theme. He could be, on occasion, terse or ample, direct or circuitous, calm or impassioned. It is, perhaps, not generally known that he was a favourite pupil of Sheridan Knowles, after that dramatist and actor became a preacher and a teacher of elocution. On the platform he was often seen to advantage, since the presence of numbers rarely failed to arouse him; and not a few public opportunities were afforded, in this country and in Canada, of declaring his strong sympathy with whatever was patriotic and progressive.

As a pastor, his own sorrows and sufferings softened and refined his nature, and made him an ever-welcome visitor when homes were darkened and hearts were sad. He could also join in wholesome relaxation and innocent mirth. At times, however, especially when burdened with some train of thought, there was an aloofness of manner, a preoccupation, which those who did not know him misinterpreted. When really at ease, he was warm, genial, frank, quick in response, and could listen as well as talk. There was a sensitiveness of nature in him which some did not suspect, a sensitiveness which increased as years rolled on. But this very feature of his character gave him great influence with others, since it aided him in the interpretation of their feelings, and in offering them counsel and comfort. His words from the pulpit, and in your homes, have stirred many hearts, and have awakened in them thoughts and impulses that will be imperishable.

And what shall I say more ? How shall I speak of the crushing blow that has fallen upon his aged mother, whom may God comfort with His own comfort and grace ? How shall I speak of the loss, beyond what words can tell, to his sisters ; to his brother, to whom he was a father ; to his wife and family ; to the people out yonder in Canada ; to the people at Brixton ; and to you who are here ? Do I not rightly interpret your feeling, especially in regard to his widow and family, when I pray that God, even their own God, and our God, would be " a father to the fatherless, and a husband to the widow " ? You know how health gave way under pressure of work upon a frame never robust. You know how entire rest did not bring relief, and that even the change back to Canada proved of no advantage.

[Mr. Goadby then gives an account of Dr. Stevenson's death, and of the funeral service, which need not here be repeated. He then concludes.]

It is something to know that his widow, who

was so much to him, his true helpmeet, and in whose resourceful care and love he found shelter, stimulus, and rest—is comforted in her grief and in the grief of her children by many letters testifying to his sympathy and care for others; and there are not a few now listening to me this night who can also bear witness to his sympathy and care, true, tender, and strong. He could help others as he did because he himself walked with God, and the Unseen was to him the real and abiding. A few more years at the most—at least, for some of us—and our end will come. Let us, then, whilst thanking God for our friend, gird up the loins of our mind, and follow him, as he followed the Master and Lord, that by and by there may be a blessed and eternal reunion in the Father's home above.

AT BRIXTON INDEPENDENT CHURCH.

The Rev. Fred Hibbert, of Newcastle-on-Tyne, who preached at Brixton on the Sunday following the arrival in England of the news of Dr. Stevenson's death, after his morning sermon paid a deep tribute to the manly sympathy and noble generousness that inspired and pervaded Dr. Stevenson and his utterances. "He was a true type of the manly Christian gentleman, which the Gospel of Jesus Christ truly understood must

always produce. I cannot speak of what he was
to you as your minister, but I can speak as a
young minister, and bear my testimony to his
intense sympathy with young souls struggling after
a greater light and a fuller truth, and to the
helpfulness of the words he sometimes spoke to
us." Mr. George Nicholls, senior deacon, read to
the congregation Mrs. Stevenson's letter giving
the sad news, and expressed the gratitude of the
church for Dr. Stevenson's inspiring ministry, and
their thankfulness that he had been spared from
possibly many years of suffering, " knowing that
he is with Christ, which is far better." At the
close of the service the whole congregation rose
spontaneously, and stood while the organ sent forth
the strains of the " Dead March " in *Saul.*

OTHER PERSONAL TRIBUTES TO DR. STEVENSON.

HENRY BLIGH JONES THUS WRITES IN *The Christian
Commonwealth* :—

A far abler hand could easily be found, but none
more loving than mine, to hastily, yet reverently,
" touch in " the character and work of my beloved
friend, whose name heads this sketch, and whom to
know was to love.

For more than five-and-twenty years it was given

me to enjoy the friendship and to witness with delight the successful career of Dr. J. F. Stevenson—
ended too soon we may think, but if we believe, as
he did, that—

"One above,
In perfect wisdom, perfect love,
Is working for the best,"

we shall feel thankful, while we mourn his loss,
that He who took him from us first gave him to us.
. . . Intensely interested in and abreast of the
urgent topics of the times, and ever welcome in
the London pulpits when occasion brought him to
the old country, he looked lovingly and longingly
on the supreme attractions which London holds
out, and accepted the honourable yet onerous
position of successor to the Rev. Baldwin Brown, at
Brixton. There his eminent qualities of heart and
mind were quickly recognized and promised long
and effective service; but a London pastorate with its
multitudinous claims, and the difficulty, from innate
kindness of heart, which he had in resisting their
pressure, soon proved too much for his strength.
A born student and thinker, no carelessness marked
his work. Any subject or science cognate to his
preaching was laid under contribution, mastered as
far as possible, and assimilated. . . .

His power was essentially that of following truth
as he saw it, and in helping truth-seekers in their
quest. Dogmatism and sectarianism had no place

in his heart. Breadth of view and the largest hope quickened his teaching and made it acceptable and valued by the young and thoughtful minds whom it was his joy and crown to help. Again and again has he spoken to me of the glad opportunities twelve years' continuous service in one sphere had afforded him, and how in that time his young friends had passed into manhood and womanhood, and the happiness he had had in forming and directing them. He was not only a helpful minister and guide, but a bright, loving, trusted friend; aiding the perplexed in the time of conflict and difficulty and doubt by his unbounded sympathy and brotherliness.

Dr. Stevenson was a true, liberal-minded Christian gentleman, tender and courteous to all; recognizing the merits of methods of Christian service which he himself did not use. I cannot forget how one Sunday morning some years ago, on his way to preach at Highbury, the sounds of the Salvation Army caught his ear. He stopped, removed his hat, and listened for a time, then with tears in his grave, sad eyes said, "Whatever others may say, who am I that I should forbid them? I *cannot*." That incident was typical of Frederick Stevenson. That spirit won its way and did its happy, noble work.

He has gone from us for "a little while"; he has joined many a friend in the city above. Professor Elmslie was at his recognition service at Brixton—they are together now, and many more; his old friend and adviser, Dr. Hannay, and other friends and workers are united there!

We shall never see him again on earth. On the last Sunday in July, 1890, he was in the City Temple, where he and his wife loved to be, and enjoyed Dr. Parker's heartfelt prayer and the sermon on the "Valley of dry bones." The doctor's application of the prophet's pathetic refrain, "O Lord, Thou knowest," was specially suited to our dear friends in their time of trial, and I could tell how often those words have comforted her who now mourns the loss of such a husband, such a life companion, as John Frederick Stevenson.

LETTER TO *The Daily Witness*, FROM DEAN NORMAN.

(To the Editor of *The Witness*.)

SIR,—I read with extreme though sad and painful interest your communication in yesterday's issue of *The Witness* (which reached me this morning), with reference to the character and life-work of my dear friend, the Rev. Dr. Stevenson. Permit me to add a few words of my own. In my judgment he was the best speaker of his day in Montreal. All who had the pleasure of knowing him can recall his choice and felicitous English, his wide literary culture, the refinement, well-nigh feminine, of his mind, and his broad and deep sympathy with all that was good and true. I enjoyed the honour of his friendship, an honour which I fully appreciate, and since his former departure from Montreal we have occasionally corresponded. Of course we had differences, but we respected one another's conscientious convictions, and both were conscious of an inner unity which nothing could break, and which bound us man to man, by the strong cords of a man. Would that there were more like him in this world! To our dim senses, it seems an inscrutable dispensation which has removed him, scarcely past the prime of life, from a loving and beloved family, from important ministerial labour, and from troops of friends. But we must bow the head in submission, and believe that the Master will have some work for His faithful servant in the other world. He will not be easily forgotten. Those eloquent and flowing words, conveyed with the charm of musical voice and scholarly accent, still linger on the ear. Let us believe that a hand of mercy has beckoned him hence, and let us be thankful that such men come among us from time to time, uplifting us from sordid employments and the strife of tongues, and pointing us to that haven of rest where, beyond these jarring earthly voices, there is peace.

I dare not speak of his family. It would be intrusive even to allude to the sacredness of their sorrow, but I desire as a former resident of Montreal, to add my testimony to the ability and the personal worth of one of whom any community might be proud, and who will, as long as life lasts, have a place in the hearts of those who knew and loved him.

R. W. Norman, D.D.

The Rectory, Quebec,
Feb. 3, 1891.

Letter from Rev. Dr. Allon.

"St. Mary's Road, Canonbury,
"*February* 24, 1891.

"Dear Mrs. Stevenson,—I was greatly startled and shocked to see the announcement in the papers of Dr. Stevenson's death. His state of health, of course, caused anxiety; but the impressions made by what we heard of him were that he was somewhat better. I need not assure you of the affectionate interest and sympathy which his sorrowful failure in health excited amongst his brethren; nor will I attempt the common consolations which I trust sustain you in your great bereavement. In such sorrows all words are cold, save His, who speaks to us as 'the Resurrection and the Life,' and who tells us of the Father's house. He can even appeal to love itself that it should assuage its sorrow. 'If ye loved me ye would rejoice, because I go unto the

Father.' And yet there was an hour of His deepest sorrow, when He sought to be 'as it were a stone's-cast from His disciples,' that He might be alone with His Father. So we feel in surroundings such as yours : sorrow we must, and sorrow we may ; nature demands it, and grace does not forbid ; to forbid sorrow were to deny affection ; only our sorrow has precious lights from God which fall upon it. It is, however, a comfort to know that, although friends are helpless, they can sympathize ; and I simply wish to assure you of this sympathy, personally enhanced as it is by many recollections of the past. May He comfort you who alone can. Upon some of us the feeling deepens, that it is but a little while 'that they are preferred before us.'

"So far as I can gather, the feeling excited by Dr. Stevenson's death has been deep and strong. His position, his character, and his abilities excited special interest, and what seems an almost untimely death has deepened it. He was highly esteemed by all his brethren, so far as my own observation went, and his loss will be felt as that of 'an able minister of Jesus Christ' and a warm-hearted brother and fellow-worker. But He has done it, who is our wise and loving Father, and we can only believe that He has done well.

"I am, my dear Mrs. Stevenson,

"Very cordially yours,

"HENRY ALLON."

LETTER FROM REV. DR. MACKENNAL.

" BOWDON, CHESHIRE,
" *February* 26, 1891.

" DEAR MRS. STEVENSON,—Mr. Flower has kindly
sent me your address, that I may write and tell
you of my personal sorrow at the loss of your
husband, and of my deep sympathy with you and
your family. As it was his own worth of character,
his frank, fresh, joyous temperament, his warm and
open heart, and his deep manliness, which made
his great charm, so all our feeling of admiration
for his attainments and gifts is overpowered by our
love for him, and that makes his death a more
poignant regret.

" I have read in the papers your little notice
of the closing scene, and I could read under it
the blending of triumph and regret which the
death must have occasioned you. He was your
husband—nothing can rob you of that joy; but
then, he *was*—the grief comes back. I hope you
can say ' *is*,' as well as ' was,' for—

" ' All that is at all,
Lasts ever, past recall.'

We were all so proud of him, and rejoiced so in
him. He seemed a new force added to our English
Congregationalism. But to me there was always
present the remembrance of that Sunday I heard
him preach in Montreal, and the communion ser-

vice which followed. I remember how, at the Lord's table, while he was speaking, his eye grew rapt, as if seeing something in the Saviour and the Supper, more than he had seen before, and then it filled with tears. I knew what it all meant, and could understand how fit for a pastor's office he was. And most of all I remember the great personal kindness with which both you and he sought me out in my suffering and gave me a tender sympathy which has always made me feel at home in Montreal. So I send you a brother's affection, and assure you of a brother's prayers. May God comfort you abundantly.

"Yours faithfully, and *his*,

"ALEXANDER MACKENNAL."

LETTER FROM REV. DR. DUFF, OF THE UNITED YORKSHIRE COLLEGE.

"ST. MARY'S ROAD, BRADFORD, YORKSHIRE,

"*March* 10, 1891.

"MY DEAR, DEAR FRIEND, MRS. STEVENSON,— May I come in a moment to your quiet now, and say my word of love? I have sat still, and felt it impossible to say anything through these months. If I could have come near, to say by the touch of the hand what words were of no use for bringing to the beloved soul in the stricken time! But that could not be, and so one had to wait. But now the wings that were all for soaring, and not for

chaining, are free again. And cannot we say to
him now, just as truly as before, all we would
say? If ever there was one to whom earth's
breast and God's breast were the same, it was he.
Blessed man! he heard the silent heaven-voices
when he was among us—heard them as so few
ever do; and surely, surely, he can hear our
souls' voices yonder, where he is, in God's bosom
now.

"It is the fair, wondrous fair beauty of him as
an oasis in my life that I keep thinking of. Beautiful soul, oh how fair! I have had a good many
rare experiences in knowing good men, noble men,
bliss-giving men; but his friendship was unique.
The acquaintance with him was the finest far. On
every side it seemed so. The beautiful sympathy
he had with me, for example, in my mathematical
work when I was in Montreal. Of course the sympathy with my Old Testament and other theological
work goes without saying. And then the sight he
had, as we walked, for the fairest things in sky and
tree and horizon. Oh, yes, he has truly been my
teacher; nay is, and ever is to be.

"I will not write on. We talk often of you.
The peace of God abide with each. Tell me if
ever I can be of any service to you over here. So
gladly would I do it.

"Faithfully ever,

"ARCHIBALD DUFF."

LETTER FROM THE REV. HARRIS CRASSWELLER (AN
OLD COLLEGE FRIEND).

"NEWPORT, FIFE, SCOTLAND,
"*February* 22, 1891.

"DEAR OLD FRIEND,—It is with very deep regret,
and with profoundest sympathy for yourself, that
I have read the sad news. I cannot put into words
what yet it lies in my heart to say. You know,
however, that I have a real and a large share in
your love, and that I cannot be without strong,
deep pity for you. There is one consolation which
will come to you—it is that you came to the difficult decision you did, and removed the dear fellow
from England while yet there was time; for if you
had not, he could not have passed his last days
with his boys as well as with you. That you must
feel now to be a large compensation for what you
had to undergo here—a compensation the more
precious because of the unutterable satisfaction it
must have been to him. . . . For tenderness and
purity I have never known F.'s superior, and hardly
ever his equal. His great gifts were under the rule
of graces greater even than they. A man? Yes!
but more than merely a man. He was a living
heart; love lived in him, and geniality and gentleness were a crown upon his strength. It is too
much to hope that he never had an enemy, but of
a truth he was no man's foe, and was every man's
lover, while forgiveness was as the breath of his

mouth. Full as his mind was, his life must have been still fuller, for plainly he burnt himself out by industry and service, and by intenseness of emotion ; and if he died before his time, it was only because his hands and his nature were alike too full. He has earned, as very few do, the proud right to be missed, now that he has left his place here, and will live for ever by what he was and by what he did. Much of its salt left the earth when he went, but not before its savour had so been felt that many had arisen to call him blessed. . . . You must pardon the poverty of these brief words. Worthier ones will not come to me just now, and would not, perhaps, even though I delayed to write. My mind is full of recollections, dating from the day when F. entered college, and running on through long years till the memorable Sunday when you so kindly fetched me to your house. How little did I think as I said ' good-bye ' to him that it was to be ' farewell.' But so it was—God knows best. . . ."

ETHICAL.

I.

TOILING IN ROWING.

"And He saw them toiling in rowing." (*Authorized Version.*)
"And seeing them distressed in rowing." (*Revised Version.*)
—MARK vi. 48.

THEY were not only working hard—there is no harm in that—but they were anxious, tortured, perplexed, and alarmed. The shadows of the night were falling, and the shore was far away. The wind was against them : it might rise into a storm. Their vessel was a small, frail boat, such as might be swamped in a moment by a heavy sea. They had foreseen all this, most likely, for we are told that they did not go very willingly. Christ had to "constrain" them, to compel them, or almost so. And you know we scarcely ever enjoy the work we do unwillingly. The art of all joy in work is to embrace it as your own—to throw yourself, your will, and your power into it. Between fear and difficulty these rowers had a hard time of it. But Christ knew all about their condition. He had meaning and purpose in what

He had done. He saw into the circumstances and
into them far better and more deeply than they
knew. And as He watched them from the shore
with wistful, loving eyes, He suffered in their
suffering ; He pitied the very toil which He saw
to be necessary, and had Himself enjoined.

One great reason of their difficulty was that
the wind was contrary. The sea dashed and
rolled against them, raised to fury by a wind
blowing against their course. I suppose you are
all able to understand what a difference that would
make. You have been in a boat when the lake
or the river was placid, and when any wind or
stream there might be was in your favour, and
you know how pleasantly the vessel glided along.
Perhaps you know also what a contrary wind can
do, how it can take away all the ease of rowing
or sailing, and turn the pleasure into pain. And
what is true of a boat on a river is true also
largely of what we often call the voyage of life.
We find the sea rough sometimes and the wind
contrary. The healthy pleasure of muscular
exercise is turned into difficulty or pain. The
task of life drags. The duty of the day seems
to be without interest, as dry and unprofitable
as dust. We look round and see other people
drifting with the sea and the wind, and ask
ourselves, Why should not we ? Why should we
take all this toil and trouble, while other men
are at ease and doing as they like ? And yet we

know we are wrong when we think so. It is a false, traitorous thought. For Christ has given the word, and, come what may, we must fulfil it. We must cross the sea and get to Bethsaida. We shall see this all the more clearly if we think of what the influences are which oppose us.

The contrary wind which opposes the command of Christ is sometimes *the power of our own inward disposition*. There is one special form of sin—our " easily-besetting sin," as the Apostle calls it—the side or aspect of our nature that seems most unguarded; where the good is weakest, and evil has its most easy entrance. You do not desire it to be thus. You look at your own character at times with something like loathing. You cry as St. Paul did, " Who shall deliver me from this body of death?" Your temptation— your special temptation I mean—seems like a dead body from which you cannot escape; repulsive, terrible, yet not to be put away. There are two selves in you, and the lower strives for mastery over the higher : the higher hates and yet cannot conquer the lower. You understand no part of the New Testament so well as you do the seventh chapter of the Romans, in which St. Paul talks of " the law in his members which wars against the law of his mind," and makes him " a captive to sin and death." I fancy there is scarcely a man now of any spiritual earnestness who has not a hundred times wished that he might

be taken to pieces and put together again after
a different and better pattern. Well, it is hard
rowing for you, my friend. The wind is contrary
and the sea is rough. But if one thing is clear
it is this—that you must row on! To give up
the struggle is to sink into a brute or a devil.
It is to throw the reins on the neck of the wild
horses and let them plunge with you over the
precipice. It is to drift out to sea and starve or
drown in the solitary ocean. The harder the
rowing the more imperative is the necessity to
row. The very purpose and meaning of life are
lost if you give up; for we are not here to grow
famous, or rich, or learned, or remarkable. We
are here to grow into harmony of character with
ourselves. We are here to make the higher
control the lower, to make conscience govern
appetite and passion, and to make Christ govern
conscience. We are here to "put away the old
man, with his affections and lusts, and to put on
the new man, who after God is created in
righteousness and true holiness." We are here
that as Christ rose again for us, so He may rise
in us, to perfect and absolute victory. And so He
will, if only *we* are true. He never abandons any
who do not of their own will abandon Him.

Another contrary wind with which we have to
contend is what I may call the *pressure of life*.
This is a matter of the modern age; almost of
the present century. Society has become ex-

cessively complicated. It touches us at a thousand points, and makes upon us extreme and continual demands. I look at the pictures of life in the country in England a century ago and almost long for some good power to put us back into it. You have all read Gray's " Elegy "—his meditation in a country churchyard. You have heard what he says of the rude forefathers of the hamlet, how they dwelt " Far from the madding crowd's ignoble strife." It seems indeed " ignoble strife " now. It may in a sense develop us. It may make us as sharp as a needle and as quick as a lightning-flash. It may give us a ready perception of all that lies on the surface of life. But it will take away the desire and the very ability for quiet and profound meditation. The modern man shines brilliantly enough on the facets of a hundred subjects. But the modern man does not *think*. Thinking is, I am afraid, becoming one of the lost arts. We talk, we write, we make money, we rush to our amusements, so that our life is a feverish, restless, morbid excitement, which fills the graveyards and the lunatic asylums: but how little we obey the precept " Commune with thine own heart, and be still." Some people like all that. There are whole cities on our continent (America) which seem to do so. The men are immersed in business schemes all the week and amuse themselves excitedly all the Sunday. You may tell me it is not so with you-

I am glad to know it. But you cannot live with
all this around you and find it as easy to live in
God and talk with Christ by the way as it would
be if such things were not true. O my brother,
try to live at home. Do not give up your Bible
and your prayer. Try to meditate on high things.
Not so much haste and hurry, I pray you! These
men on the sea were under the eye of their
Master. So are you and I. And we are bound
under penalties to remember Him. I say this age
is forgetting God. Many of our intellectual men
are doing so avowedly. They are angry if we call
them Atheists, and yet they are doing all they
can to blot out from science, from literature and
life the very idea of the Father of Spirits. And
what they do in theory thousands more do in
practice. But "oh the pity of it, the pity of
it!" Poor, miserable, cramped, narrow, and
hopeless is life without God. St. Paul is right;
"without God" is "without hope in the world."
Yes, and the still older writer is right too: it is
"the *fool* who hath said in his heart, There is no
God." If you let this life press the spiritual life
out of your hearts be sure the day of reckoning
will come. The pitcher will be broken at the
fountain, and the wheel broken at the cistern,
your science or fashion will give you joy no longer,
and you will long in vain for a peace and a
communion which you now thrust away with
supercilious disdain or restless impatience. God

sees you, and the day will come when you will awake, and for good or for evil will see God.

The voyage of life is made difficult also by *personal trial and sorrow.* These will be sure to come. I cannot enumerate their forms, however briefly; but I may say that it seems to me that in this respect also our life grows more complicated. I do not say we suffer more, but life is, I think, more clouded with anxiety and apprehension than it used to be. Business is uncertain, and often, I am afraid, not really sound. Men are too much in debt and too speculative. Poverty is more possible to the comfortable and even to the rich, and the poor amongst us are burdened with care. They are often perplexed where to look or what to do for the next meal. Sickness, too, is often joined with poverty; partly it is the cause and partly the result of it. Oh, it is a terrible "toiling in rowing" when a poor woman, half dead of some destructive disease, has to work from dawn to dark for a scanty meal for her children and herself, or when a man drags to his heavy task limbs racked with pain or disjointed and deformed by former accident. Harder still perhaps is it for a strong man, willing to work, to find the work itself denied him.

" O God, protect us," sang the Brittany fishermen, as they gazed across the ocean ; " Thy sea is so large, and our boats are so small." And if

Christ looks on you and me He must see us often as He saw His followers of old *toiling* as we guide our frail vessel over the stormy sea. And yet these very sorrows are among the strongest reasons why we cannot do without Him. The contrary wind and the stormy sea cry out for Christ, with a strong and pathetic cry. He grasps the only power which can control both them and us. He alone can at once quiet our terrors and calm the storm-tossed billows.

Look at these men as they toil upon the waters. They are all taken up with their efforts, and know of nothing but that. But the fact is they are not left to themselves. *He saw* them. Even taken alone there is an infinite help and comfort in that. Love and care are a world of comfort to us, even when they bring no direct relief but the knowledge of their own existence. You see we live not alone and apart, but in each other; so that the mere sense of sympathy is new life and strength to us. We want a human touch— the touch of a man's hand and a man's heart. The fact that Christ saw them would have been life to them if they had known it. It would have brought the consciousness of society and the certainty of help. But they did not know it. As they toiled on the sea it was to them as though they had been utterly alone. "Alone, alone, all, all alone," alone on a wide, wild sea. So they seemed to be. I am glad of this incident in the

Gospels, because it is, as I may say, a little engraving on a gem, or a minute photograph which gives us in a small space the Divine plan of our lives. We toil; God watches. We are afraid; He is calm, for He holds wind and wave in the hollow of His hand. We cry for help; there is no voice nor any that answereth. Yet the help is near: ready, waiting for the right moment and the right way. It does not come too soon. It leaves us to struggle, to doubt, and almost to fail, nay, sometimes quite to fail. Yet it is there. And if it does not come too soon, so neither will it ever come too late. You who live the spiritual life with difficulty, look to that. You will get through. You may be battered and bruised; you may be storm-tossed and weary; you may be ready to perish; but hold on:

"His wisdom conducts thee, His power defends;
In safety and quiet thy voyage He ends."

I think life would not be possible to earnest men without such a faith as that. It applies to our individual lives. But not only so; it applies to the wider life of the world. The course of the world's history is often discouraging and distressing enough. It seems as though it were like a railroad train thrown off the track and rushing to its ruin.

Atheism, godless indifference, devotion to the poorer and meaner purposes of life, the influx

into our cities of all the elements of disorder
and disturbance, Irish disloyalty, German unbelief,
and everywhere debauchery and riot ; and you and
I lifting up here and there what seems a solitary
voice for Christ and for God! How is it all to
end ? *Is* Christ dead ? Has His name lost its
power ? Did He go out like a beautiful vision and
leave only the memory of a lovely dream when
He died on the cross, "while o'er His grave the
Syrian stars look down " ? Or is there energy
in His gospel still ? Will His kingdom come?
Shall the wilderness and the solitary place be glad
for Him, and the desert rejoice and blossom as
the rose ? I read the answer in such passages
as my text. Christ loved these men. He put
them to no meaningless or needless pain. He was
not only ready and willing, He was eager to help.
So He is now. But He saw them as they could
not see themselves. He saw issues of the present,
stretched out into a boundless and a complicated
future. And He made no haste. He let events
work themselves out, till men wanted Him and
knew that it was He whom they wanted. Then
He came. Even then, however, He came, not as
they might have expected Him, but in a new and
unfamiliar form. He walked on the sea, not
apparently the Jesus whom they knew, but like
a ghost, an apparition, something to startle and
to amaze them. It may be so again. The Christ
who comes to you and me in the future may not

at first sight look like the Christ whom we have long and lovingly known. We may have to see Him from a different side and appreciate Him in a different aspect. He may come in pain, in want, in remorse, in agony. And so of the world. The gospel of the future may not sound in all respects as the gospel of the past has done. It may lay its emphasis in a different place and hold up a salvation fuller and more many-sided than former days required. But O my brothers, Christ is coming. He will be your Saviour and Friend— He and none but He. He will come on board the boat, whether it be the boat which carried your individual destiny, or that which bears the future of the whole race of men. And when He comes the winds and the waves will cease, "and immediately there will be a great calm." "Even so—come Lord Jesus!"

II.

DRIFTING.

"For let not that man think that he shall receive anything of the Lord; a double-minded man is unstable in all his ways."—JAMES i. 7, 8.

SOCIETY is full of such men. We meet them at the corner of every street; in all our houses of business; at every evening party; and wherever men "most do congregate." They have nothing to think, and they think it. They have nothing to say, and they say it, though they may talk all day long. They have nothing to do, and they do it. How can it be otherwise when they *are* nothing in particular? I am sometimes told of such men, that there is "no harm in them." And yet to be nothing may be a very harmful thing. Nothing, indeed, can do no good, but it may be a fruitful source of evil. Death is negation; it is mere absence of life; but absence of life soon becomes decay and corruption.

There may be some such men here to-night. Poor waves of the sea, scattered in spray, or dashed to pieces on the shore! I wish to speak to such men, not in ridicule or harshness, but in all brotherly sincerity and earnestness.

Consider, then, what this state of mind is. I call it "drifting." The text calls it doubting, or wavering, or double-mindedness. "Men of two souls," as it is literally.

A young man comes to me—for everybody takes his troubles and perplexities to the minister, and I am very glad he does, for if a minister ceases to be helpful and sympathetic he belies his name— a young man comes to me and says :—

"I have had a good education, I want to be a tutor."

"Well, what do you know?"

"Oh, I know a little Latin and Greek, and something of mathematics and history."

"Have you done any teaching?"

"No, I can't say that I have."

"What makes you think you are fit for that?"

"Well, I went in for medicine, but I did not like it; in fact I failed to pass my exams."

"Did you try anything else?"

"Yes, I tried a merchant's office; but a clerk's position does not suit me, I find the hours long and the work very monotonous."

"So you think you are fit for teaching, do you, because you are not fit for anything else? You can train other minds although you have never trained your own? You think you can go through life without doing disagreeable things? Believe

one who knows, when I tell you that you cannot.
If you are to be fit for anything you must 'endure
hardness,' as the good old Book says. You must get
up early when you would far rather lie and rest.
You must do dry, uninteresting work, when it
would be far more fascinating to read romances
or dream under the trees; you must meet surly,
disagreeable people and talk to them kindly and
respectfully; and, above all, you must work, work,
work, whether you like it or no, if you mean to
succeed in life. If that sounds harsh, I am sorry;
but it is not so harsh as it sounds. No, thank
God! Only begin, and the labour which seemed
but a curse shall become a sacrament. Be a man,
not a log of driftwood; and before you know it,
the dry study will be radiant with interest, and the
dreary work full of fascination."

The principle of which I am speaking applies,
however, especially to our religious life. A man
who hesitates and drifts in religion is lost. This
is the great temptation of our day. Many of you
are without any clear convictions, and without
any definite aim in religion. A score of different
views are advocated on all the great questions.
The very air is full of speculation and debate.
The Reviews discuss the problems of life and
destiny. The Monthly Magazines are oracular
concerning them. Even the Daily Papers toss
them lightly about, so that we may read a para-
graph in the column of varieties on the being of

God, or the immortality of the soul, while we are breaking an egg at breakfast or sipping our afternoon tea. I do not altogether regret this. It would not matter if I did, for the fact is here, and it will not depart at any man's bidding. And the consequences of the fact are here too. The greatest of all questions, those that enter *most* deeply into character and destiny, are apt to be regarded as matter of merely intellectual interest, like the squaring of the circle or the constitution of a star. And so it happens that some of you, with high mental gifts, are sailing in the pleasure-boat of your own thoughts round the whole world of speculation and casting anchor nowhere.

My friends, are you going to settle every speculation before you begin to *live!* For time is passing on winged feet while you are dreaming. To what single thing can you point which you have really done, which shall bear fruit unto everlasting life? "Be not deceived, God is not mocked; whatsoever a man soweth, that shall he also reap." And this is true not for ourselves alone, but for others. "For no man liveth to himself, and no man dieth to himself." We cannot be saved without saving others, nor lost without destroying others, if it be only by our neglect. Amidst a thousand things we do not know, we have yet sufficient light for "life and godliness." You must accept some central view of life if you are to be anything but a poor waif and stray. As Mr.

Huxley says, you must have a "working hypo-
thesis." Grant me at least as much as this: that
right is better than wrong; truth better than falsehood; goodness than evil. Believe, then, in these;
and, that they may be *realities* to you and not
mere abstract names, believe in the God in whom
they eternally exist, and in the Christ in whom
they are made manifest to men. "If any man
will do my Father's will he shall know of the
doctrine," says the Saviour. It is said that religious truth cannot be verified. We are told that
it cannot be proved by experiment. I maintain
that it can. For is not the verification of a promise its fulfilment? Is not the proof of a salvation
the fact that it saves? I challenge this proof for
my Saviour, Christ. For "we have not followed
cunningly devised fables when we made known
unto you the power and coming of our Lord Jesus
Christ." "We know in whom we have believed."
Of all certainties none is so certain as personal
character, when once it has been tried and proved.
And, beloved, some of us have *proved* our Saviour.
A thousand times ten thousand, even thousands
of thousands have set to their seal that He is true.

Vacillation, of course, implies weakness. A
wavering mind will never fulfil the Apostle's in-
junction to "quit you like men, *be strong.*"
Virility, manliness, is impossible to such a nature;
heroism, an "unknown quantity." General Grant
used to say that he went trembling into his first

battles ; but he was not long in discovering that if
he feared others, others also feared him. " I soon
found," he tells us, " that the true question for a
soldier is not what the enemy intends to do to him,
but what he intends to do to the enemy." A brave
man is not continually thinking about what others
say or do. He has laid plans of his own. Once
having done so, he carries them out with all his
energies. " Immediately I conferred not with
flesh and blood," says the brave Apostle to the
Gentiles. I did not hesitate, nor complain, nor
long for case, nor consult others ; I saw the right
as by a lightning-flash, and I went and did it. A
man with a soul can respect a character like that.
A man who does not respect it is on his way to
become a coward. Indeed, this little man Paul,
whom we have quoted, is a grand lesson in steadfastness of purpose. With his bodily presence
weak, and his speech contemptible, he nevertheless
moved the world to its centre, and lives a mighty
power amongst us to-day. All great men have
possessed this faculty of unswerving fixity of
purpose. Above all it was the characteristic of
" the Man " Christ Jesus. He " set his face
steadfastly to go up to Jerusalem," though He
knew it meant desertion, betrayal, crucifixion ; the
last and supremest sacrifice. Had He faltered or
shrunk back on that terrible road, where would
have been our faith and hope to-day ? And the
religion of Jesus, while it can adapt itself to the

wants of the weakest, is, in its spirit and temper, a religion to test the mettle of the strongest man.

Be men, then, ye who listen to me. Vacillation, instability, is fatal to character and disastrous to life. The world is full of poor sickly creatures who could have done noble work had they dared to face and vanquish obstacles. I can trace the failure of many whom I have personally known to the lack of a definite purpose. I go so far as to say that our criminal classes are largely re-cruited by such as these: waifs and strays who are the sport of circumstances, driven by the winds and tossed—with no moral backbone, as we say. And the beginning seemed almost innocent. A song and a glass, a glass and a song, and then another and another, just because others asked for it. That was how it commenced, and now the man is a drunken wreck. Or a little debt, carelessly incurred, or a few pence from the till, which you quite intended to replace. But it drifted into theft, and forgery, and then sudden detection, shame unutterable, and a blasted career. A look of impure love—just one—and then—ah! we dare not dwell on it;

> " But there followed a mist and a blinding rain,
>   And life was never the same again."

They mean no harm, they tell me ; and I believe it. But God is telling us in a hundred ways that we must mean His will if we are truly to live, and mean it with all the energy of our being. We must lay hold of His unswerving purpose if we are to be saved.

And what I have been saying applies to you, my sisters, too. Oh! the vacant, foolish, characterless women I have known. Wives and mothers who have never risen to the dignity that God has laid upon them, whose homes testify to their neglected opportunities. Poor wasted lives are these; spiritual forces flung away. And when we think of the infinite good a woman can be, and of her measureless influence, we are ready to cry out with pain when we see what she sometimes becomes.

Men and women, are you drifting—waves of the sea, driven with the wind and tossed? Perhaps so. Some of you may have lost all power, and almost all desire, to do anything else. When you look into the world of " might-have-been," you are for a moment saddened and ashamed. But nothing stimulates you to fresh endeavour. A mocking spirit whispers in taunting accents, " Too late, I tell you ; it is too late." No, it is not too late ! That is only one more of the devil's lie which have made you what you are. It is never too late to do better in a world where Christ has lived and died. Greater is He that is for you than all that are against you. He speaks to-night through these poor lips of mine, commanding you to come to Him. If you are feeble, He is strong; if you are weak and wavering, He is " the same yesterday, and to-day, and for ever," and all His strength and love and steadfastness are pledged to save you. Only, I beseech you, come to Him now. I had almost ventured to say, " Now or never." For it is just this that makes the subtle, the awful fatality of drifting. You are deferring and still deferring to decide, till even the desire for better things will have perished. It is growing more and more difficult *not* to drift. Of you it is emphatically true, " Now is the accepted time, now is the day of salvation."

III.

THE WHITE STONE AND THE NEW NAME.

"And will give him a white stone, and in the stone a new name written, which no man knoweth saving he that receiveth it."—REV. ii. 17.

THIS promise is given to the Church at Pergamos. To understand it we ought to remember the peculiar temptations to which that church was exposed—what its members would have to conquer. The city was an idolatrous one, and though, when once Christ had been fully known and accepted, it was perhaps impossible that men should return again to their idolatry, yet they were exposed to the moral laxity, the elegant and unblushing corruption which hovered in the very air. The church had been firm and bold in its confession of Christ. Antipas, the faithful martyr, had sealed his testimony with his blood. But was it necessary, some were asking, to go to such an extreme? Why should they be so rigid and unyielding in their temper? Some were inclined to a compromise. Why be sour and ungenial? The great difficulty was in social intercourse with the

heathen around them. Many of these heathen
were amongst their old friends. Might they not
dine with them ? And if some heathen customs
came into the feast, what were they to do? Paul
had dealt with these matters before, and John does
so here. Their principle is the same. Do nothing
that defiles your conscience, or that can cause
other people to fall. Ask no impertinent questions
on the one hand; on the other, do not eat what
you know has been offered to idols ; and, above all
things, keep yourselves in the purity of Christ.
Surly you need not be; but true to God, and true
to Christian chastity, you must. Then comes the
promise. "He that overcometh" shall have the
reward suited to his consistency. He has foregone
the impure delicacies at the splendid feasts of
worldly men. But he shall eat of the hidden
manna—the sacred food laid up in the golden vessel
in the ark, hidden in the Holy of Holies. Christ
is the sacred food which came down from heaven,
and is gone thither again. He has entered into
the true Shekinah. The victor soul shall be
nourished—here in part, and hereafter perfectly—
on Him.

Then we have these mystical words of my text,
"I will give him a white stone, and in the stone a
new name written, which no man knoweth save he
that receiveth it." Strange words, I say—a sort of
spiritual enigma; yet not without blessed meaning. Such language has, as a matter of course,

received different interpretations. Some have said that the white stone means acquittal, because a white pebble or bean was dropped into the vase by those who voted " not guilty" in the ancient courts of justice. Some, again, believe that it means reward, because such a stone was given to those who conquered in the races. But we must bear in mind that this Book of Revelation does not deal in Greek or Roman imagery, and those of which I speak were Gentile customs. All the figures of this book are drawn from the sacred oracles of the Jews, and from them alone. And then, what of the new name? There was no name on the pebbles that were used for acquittal or reward. But here is a name—a name which no man knoweth save him who receiveth the stone.

I think we must see here not acquittal merely, not even reward, but *revelation*. The stone is a priestly figure. It is the bright, colourless stone called " Urim," or " Thummim," or both, which the priest carried inside the folds of the breast-plate. That had a name upon it—the unspeakable name of God. Both the stone and the name flashed out in radiant splendour when the priest went into the holy place to receive the Divine word. So that the reward of the conqueror in our text is a priestly reward. He shall eat of the hidden manna, where it is laid up in the sacred place; he shall receive the Divine name on the glistening jewel of special revelation. The first thing that strikes us, on looking at the wider aspects of a text like this, is that revelation depends on character. The name on the stone is unknown and unintelligible to every one but to him who receives it. He only can see it; he only can read it. We often feel that it would be a glorious thing if God would draw near and reveal Himself to us more fully. Oh, if we could know Him as He is, how would our souls glow and burn within us! One glance at Him would chase away the misery of our sin and the loneliness of our lives. We should see, as George Fox saw when he said that there were two oceans before him—an ocean of darkness and death, and an ocean of light and life; and he beheld, and lo! the ocean of light and life flowed over and swallowed up the ocean of sin and death. God would be the great fact to us; all things would be full of Him. But we are apt to forget that it is only under certain conditions that it is possible for God to reveal Himself. We cannot see without a clear eye, nor hear unless our ear be sensitive and finely tuned. We cannot receive the highest spiritual truth unless we are in a condition to feel and to comprehend it. It is not too much to say that God cannot reveal the secrets of His heart except to those who are prepared for them. Spiritual truth is for the spiritual eye. Open our eyes, Lord, that we may see, and then give us a vision of Thyself!

We live in an age when this prayer is specially

needed : an age when the very essence of all faith and hope—the being of a God who is love and righteousness—is sifted and debated on every hand. I do not think this question will be settled by debate. If we cannot accept the revelation of God in Christ I know not where we shall look for Him. This is the condemnation—that Light has come into the world, and men have deliberately chosen darkness. "Believe me," pleads the Saviour, in tender, beseeching tones—"believe that I am in the Father, and the Father in me." "He that hath seen Me hath seen the Father." If any of you ask for a revelation of God I point you to the Man Christ Jesus. By His agony and bloody sweat, by His cross and passion, by His death and resurrection, behold in that Divine sacrifice of suffering Love the nature and the revelation of the Deity. For myself I can no more doubt Christ than I can doubt my mother's love or my father's goodness, and I have yet to hear of those who have trusted Him finding Him to fail. Rather are they ready to exclaim with one who left all for Him long ago, "*I know* whom I have believed, and am persuaded that He is able to keep that which I have committed unto Him even unto the end!"

Notice, again, that God prepares us to receive the revelation of Himself through personal trial and discipline. "To him that *overcometh.*" What a hailstorm of trial and temptation that word "over-cometh" implies! How much has entered into the

life-history and education of the man that overcometh! That is a great word—education. I
believe it to be the key to the mysteries of our
life and experience. I think it all means that God
is training and fitting us for something greater and
better. And if so, it is full of hope for us. We
can bear anything, you know, if we are sure that
good is to come out of it. I have known a feeble
woman lie for an hour on the operating-table of an
hospital, writhing under the surgeon's knife, every
nerve throbbing with the acutest agony, because
she hoped for health as the result of the operation.
What do not men go through,—put *themselves*
through,—to gain knowledge and skill in science,
or literature, or art? If it is all part of a development, if it has new power and higher life as the
outcome of it, nothing is too hard to bear. Even
evil, which is a step to good, loses its worst character as evil. The "soul of goodness" shines
through the body of repulsiveness and transfigures
it. We take the dark beginning for the sake of the
glorious end, and rejoice in the whole together.
Have not Reformers and Martyrs kissed the rack
and rejoiced in the flames, and the headsman's axe,
because they saw that liberty and truth would
arise to their successors out of the tragedy of
their pain? Even the Captain of our salvation
"endured the cross, despising the shame for the
joy that was set before Him." Oh, yes, let us see
an end, a purpose, a meaning in our suffering, and

we will not complain! If I am sure that the cross is leading to the crown, I will wreathe the cross with flowers.

And now see how this idea of a Divine education lends hope and purpose to our lives. We are apt to think of them as poor and mean. And so they often are. But if Omnipotent Love is educating us, what does the meanness matter? It will all turn to grandeur some day. Think of the power of education even as we see it. What is this in my hand? A common, brown, ugly little seed. But let the sun, and the air, and the dew educate it, and what will it become? A flower so lovely that no poet's imagination could have dreamt it; or a grand oak-tree of the forest, with its mighty life. The very world itself is the result of an education. It was "without form, and void," till God educated it into order, and developed it into beauty. If so, He may make something even out of you and me. We are infants now, and sickly, puny infants, too; but the skill of the Divine Father may unfold us "into the stature of men in Christ Jesus." Courage, weak soul, there are better things in store for you than you have yet the faith to believe! The glorious sunlight was only a cold, grey streak of dawn at first, and the little glimmer of spiritual life in you now shall shine "more and more unto the perfect day."

The "mystery of pain," then, is largely solved for us. Even sin loses part of its puzzle if through

it, and by it, God is training us all. It is permitted
that it may be conquered. Innocence is beautiful—
innocence, I mean, that has never been tempted—
but holiness that has conquered temptation is
infinitely nobler. If life be education I can well
believe that God will cause even the sins and
errors of men " to praise Him, and the remainder
thereof He will restrain."

And so the secret of life is this overcoming.
And those who know the meaning of life are able
to read the name—the new name of God—on the
white stone. We can understand just so much of
God as our experience reveals to us, and no more.
He does not change, of course. But there are
aspects and sides of His character known only to
those who have passed through special phases of
discipline. God has as many names as He has
faithful children ; and each of these names can be
read by him, and by him alone, who has been
specially trained to read it.

And now look for a moment at *the end and
purpose of all.this effort and training.* It is that
we may be like God : " partakers of the Divine
nature." No one can read the new name but he
to whom the stone is given. Why can he read
it ? Because his character fits him to read it.
And why does his character fit him to read it ?
Because it has become like God in the special
aspects expressed by the name. Like to like, you
know, all the world over. Air to the atmosphere,

the drop to the ocean, the iron to the magnet, the flower to the sunlight. So the new name of God —His " new, best name of love "—comes to him who is like it. You can read souls, some of you. You know what it is to enter a room, and look into a face, and feel that you understand what those eyes are saying. There is something kindred in that soul to yours. You can read it because you are like it. You have a life in common with it. That is why he that overcometh can read the name of God on the white stone. And it puts, in a word, all the purpose of the dealings of God with you and me. He wants us to be so like Him that we shall read His name, enter into His plans, sympathize with His spirit, make His purpose our own, mingle the little stream of our life with the infinite ocean of His. That is what He sent His Son to do for us. It is what Christ longs to do— to make us one with God. This losing of our own will and thought in the will and thought of God is, in fact, the finding of our true selves. Let me, then, read the new name on the white stone ; spell it out letter by letter, now, O God, till in its full revelation I find my heaven at last !

IV

GOD'S GENTLENESS MAN'S GREATNESS.

"Thy gentleness hath made me great."—Psa. xviii. 35.

THIS psalm is ascribed to David. It is written in memory of the great mercy whereby he had been rescued from the jealousy of Saul as well as from the Philistines. The word translated "gentleness" is one very remarkable as applied to God. It means strictly "meekness" or "lowliness." It is full, therefore, of that delicate sense of the nearness of God to man which runs, as a sort of gospel before Christ, through the nobler and sweeter parts of the Old Testament. Can the Mightiest delight in meekness? The psalmist dimly thought He could. It seemed to him that in some way the highest and the lowliest must meet and be one in God. God must be the meeting-point of all spiritual excellence, even in its extremest forms of contrast. Wonderful was it that he had so deep, so Divine an insight. But to us this truth is not doubtful. Nay, thank God, so familiar is it that it is almost a commonplace. Christ is the union of the highest and the humblest. He is gentle as a little child. And this gentleness it is that lies at the foundation of all our power.

It is this that makes us great. It is a wonderful fact that no other religion has a God whose great characteristic is gentleness. The gods of the nations have been made very much in the image of the makers. They are the gods of a rude time, a rough state of society. They are therefore rough and rude themselves. They are drawn from the fierce and terrible aspects of nature. They hurl thunderbolts, and pierce the corners of the sky with forked lightning. They make men shiver with affright. In the Bible only have we a gentle God. But, mark me, gentleness is strong. For what is gentleness? It is the quality by which purposes are reached by indirect means. Gentleness carries out its designs. But it allows time. It gives play to the mind and will of others. It is never impatient, hurried, confused. It moves quietly along, bending all circumstances to its blessed influence. The dawn—"the dayspring from on high"—is gentle. Yet the dawn is the source of all the power we know. Force, as we call it, is sunlight in an altered form. And the administration of God is full of gentleness. Everywhere we find quiet growth and slow, progressive activity. God delights in delicate handling. He is patient. He waits for results, and keeps His might in the background.

The tendency to believe in acts of bare power has sometimes corrupted theology. God has been conceived as deciding all things by the mere omnipotence of His will. He did this or that simply because He chose to do it, apart from the question whether or no it was right or reasonable. Nay, some have gone so far as to say that He made things right merely by willing that they should be done. They have not considered that by doing so they have taken away all ground for honouring God for His goodness. Bare power is the God of many even to-day. "Might is right," and He strikes here, or thunders there, performing the work of a giant on a larger scale, to "split the ears of the groundlings." To such a view the very love of God becomes arbitrary favouritism, and heaven and hell not the necessary results of character, but awards given in an artificial, wilful way.

Now, mark me, I am not denying the power of God. His forbearance would be only weakness if there were not the background of His almighty will behind. It is just because of His almightiness that His gentleness is so strength-giving. He bears with us, guides us, trains us, but He does not abdicate His authority. He is on the throne still. You know that even a woman's gentleness, if we are to respect it, must keep the steady hand

within the velvet glove. It must unite in itself
varied forms of power. She must have—

"The reason firm; the temperate will;
Endurance, foresight, strength, and skill;
A perfect woman, nobly planned,
To warn, to comfort, to command."

This is the gentleness that gathers round it the
honour of husband, brother, or son. It is great
itself, and it makes others great.

But does God in fact take the method of this
persuasive and gentle dealing with men? Look
at some proofs of it. Scripture is full of illustrations of this truth. Adam falls; but in the midst
of his ruin and punishment God's love is weaving
and working his redemption. "Exceeding great
and precious promises" comfort him in spite of
his sin. He is taken up into the arms of a
constant daily Providence; sent out into the world
to gather experience, but never deserted by the
watchful love of God. He is the God of Joseph
too, and not only of Joseph, but of his less worthy
brothers. The famine falls on them; they and
their little ones are pinched with hunger. And
then we see how God's merciful purpose has been
ripening through all the changes in Joseph's life,
and he is made the saviour of the whole family.
Look again at the passage through the desert.
The people are a horde of slaves at the outset, but
by the long and loving discipline of God they are

changed into "freemen of the Lord." How wonderfully were they plied with mercy and miracle,
with discipline and forbearance, with victory and
defeat! The whole gospel, it is plain, goes on the
same plan. The gospel is a religion of law,
though of law dissolved in love. There is no
abolition of law. By the terrible law of consequences the results of men's sin gather on the
head of Christ upon the cross. Yet the gospel comes
to us not as penalty but as pleading mercy. If
it shows us the awfulness of sin it shows us also
the unchanging love of God, beseeching us to
turn away from evil and to be reconciled to Him.
We see the face of God, against whom we have
sinned, and behold, it does not flash with anger
and just indignation—it is radiant with redeeming
love. See the "gentleness which makes us great,"
manifest in the cross of Jesus, and see it there
as you can see it nowhere else. It is the great
revelation of the Father's heart.

We may see this gentleness, too, running like a
golden thread through all our lives. How long
God has borne with us! His providence is an
elaborate plan by which we are allowed to discover
the evil of sin and the joy of goodness. We begin
by trying to go our own way. God checks and
circumvents us, till we find to our surprise that
we are going His way. It is like the story of
Jonah, who ought to go to Nineveh, but who goes
to Joppa, in exactly the opposite direction; yet

he finds himself at Nineveh, after all. Much like this is the story of many a young man. He is wilful and headstrong. He seems to be left to himself and allowed to reap the fruit he has sown. But he cannot come down to the husks that the swine do eat without being reminded of the bread in his father's house. For all know the sequel: the home-coming and the father's love; the best robe and the jewelled ring; the feasting and joy. "Thy gentleness hath made me great," must be the cry of many a returning wanderer.

Why is all this? What is God doing with us? He is obviously not alone, or even chiefly, getting His own will merely *as* His own. He could do that with the greatest ease. He could compel us to an absolute submission in a hundred ways. Why, then, does He adopt this method? The text answers. *He is making us great.* He is not crushing our nature, but training us into nobleness and power. Now observe carefully that this is what God desires: He desires to make us great. But does not God humble us? Does He not make us feel our littleness and nothingness? Yes, He does. He does desire to make us feel our weakness so long as we are apart from Him. But that is not His ultimate purpose. It could give God no pleasure to make us feel poor and mean. He only does so as the first step to a higher end. He desires to make us conscious of the grandeur of our capacities, the splendour of our nature, when we are one with Him. He makes us feel our weakness that He may show us our true strength. He will have large, free, noble souls to serve Him. He will fill them with light and equip them with power. God designs us to embody the fulness of the stature of manhood in Christ Jesus. He would take the spiritual part of us—*the will*—and set it free. He desires to see that lordly power become glorious and great. A will given to God is at once made invincible to all beside. "We fear God, and therefore we fear no one else," said a great man. And the Apostle Paul says the same in other words. He tells us that in watchings and fastings, in cold and famine, in stripes and imprisonments, his will was fixed. "Saints, apostles, prophets, martyrs," say the same thing. Thousands of wills are growing strong in Christ now, growing as the tree grows, imperceptibly but irresistibly. God would have us strong in intellect too. Therefore it is that the problems of the world and of life are so puzzling and obscure. It is not truth, but the search after truth, which makes the mind strong and clear. Therefore God sets us to think. He gives us puzzle and problem, not so much to baffle us, as that we may ultimately reach, and acquire strength to bear, the fulness and grandeur of the completed truth. He would have us live among great thoughts because we have to live with Him!

So, too, of all other noble affections, and of all the other elements of greatness. God would have our character unfold into vast and harmonious proportions, so that it may catch and reflect the image of His own. This is why He takes so long with us. This explains the severities of life: perplexity, poverty, pain, disappointment, loss. These are the stones by which He is building up His living temple. Out of weakness He is making us strong, out of poverty He is giving us wealth. When you can bear the disappointments of life peacefully and strongly you are growing great. Men and women, do not be voluntarily little. Put on the greatness of Christ; for Christ is the incarnate gentleness of God, and He shall make you great!

V.

POWER IN A ROBE.

MARK v. 25–34.

WE may be sorry for this poor woman. She was one of those of whom there are many in the world, who can neither live nor die. She dragged on a weary, miserable existence. In her worst moments, perhaps, she had prayed, "Lord, let me die; in mercy put an end to my wretched pain, and still more wretched weakness, and take me to Thyself; for Thou livest, and if I can but get to Thee I shall live too." She had been to many physicians; "but," says Mark, with a touch of irony, "she was nothing better, but rather grew worse." At length she heard of Jesus. She scarcely dared to hope that He could do anything for her case. Yet He looked kind and gentle; He had helped and healed others, and she resolved to try. It would be too much to meet Him face to face. Timid and unnerved with the peculiar character of her disease, she shrank from the eyes of men. Perhaps, however, He would not notice her amongst the crowd which thronged Him. But touch Him she must and would. In some dim way she felt that He was the Healer; the power was in Him, and could go forth from Him; so she said, "If I may but touch the hem of His garment I shall be made whole."

She was right. Her woman's instinct had not deceived her. The power of Christ was there. She touched Him, and was healed! And then the Lord turned and looked upon her. She was afraid, and yet with a fear that drew her to Him, instead of driving her away. There is no refuge *from* infinite wisdom and love, except *to* infinite wisdom and love. The disciples, as usual, were groping in the dark, and were well nigh ridiculing the Master for questioning who had touched Him. But the healed woman knew full well, and she knew that concealment was impossible, so she fell at Jesus' feet and told Him all the truth. Then He spoke. She received a word as well as a look, and a touch of power; and the word was tender and strong: "Daughter, thy faith hath made thee whole; go in peace, and be whole of thy plague." So she was healed by a touch, and that the touch of a garment. Can we understand it? Fully, no. In part I think we may. Garments are wonderful things. They seem to become a part almost of the very person of the wearer. They catch something of the impalpable influence that flows out from us to those who know and love us. Those who have lost a little child know what a world of tender feeling may gather round a tiny shoe, or baby frock. Every lover knows how precious is a tress of hair or even a knot of ribbon that formed part of the personality of the beloved. I do not explain it. I shall be told that it is all the work of association, and that very fanciful; but I believe it is more. There is a real outflow of power from us all, and a real receiving of the power by the objects that are in close contact with us. It was so with Christ. Virtue, power, flowed into and through His garment. Touching that was touching Him, and that was life and joy. His power was perfect and Divine, —ours is human and defective,—there is the great difference. The law it followed was the law of personal life, which diffuses around its own character, and heals or injures according to its quality.

Now it seems to me that Christ does for you and me very much what He did for this poor woman. He has His garments now, by which, if we touch them, He heals us.

> " The healing of His seamless dress
>   Is by our beds of pain :
> We touch Him in life's throng and press,
>   And we are whole again."

" His touch hath still its ancient power." He grants us a look, a Divine word, as He did this poor woman, and we, too, are healed. And in our smaller measure we do the same for others, in proportion as we are filled by His Spirit.

Look, now, at some of the garments of Christ which we may touch and be healed. In one view they are as simple as the robe He wore when He was upon earth; in another view they are a right royal clothing.

Theology, as we call it, is one of the garments of Christ. It makes a very variegated robe, a "coat of many colours." Like Joseph's coat, too, it has sometimes been stripped away from its owner altogether, and dyed in blood, treacherously and cruelly. For theology is the thought of men about Christ, and it has been varied and diverse as their many minds; and sometimes there has been in it little of the Divine love and graciousness of the Saviour, and much, very much, of the harshness and materialism of men. And yet Christian theology is often a rich and royal robe—a robe full of spiritual power. St. Paul has helped to weave it, and he was no pigmy. St. John also; and you know the great painters draw his portrait as that of a mighty man, with an eagle near him holding his pen. Even beyond the Bible there have been giants of the race of theologians. Augustine was one, Chrysostom was another, Aquinas and Scotus others still; nor must we omit the calm Melancthon, the profound Calvin, clear and cold as the morning light, and the rich and varied splendours of Hooker and Jeremy

Taylor. They wove a robe for Christ of lofty and far-reaching thought, and reverently folded it around His Divine form. Power was in it, and is still. Hundreds of people sneer at theology to-day who would look very small in the hands of one of these mighty theologians. Of course they were not infallible. Time has developed their mistakes. In some respects we can never again think exactly in their grooves. Yet they may help us if we will. Their theology was a robe for *Christ*, and He never changes. The garment may grow old in time and new ones supersede them, but "*He* is the same yesterday, and to-day, and for ever." And we must remember how many men and women have touched the old garments in their time, and have been healed by Christ through His robe. The thoughts of these mighty men have been channels of grace to many. Jesus was in them, and He poured Himself through them. And even now there is a tender interest and a thrilling power lingering about them.

If we do not read the works of the old divines in all respects to form our opinions, we may still do so to inspire our hearts and to stimulate our love. Whatever dress Christ has ever worn to any true man has always something of Christ in it. For my part I love these dear old divines. Hooker is dear to me, and Baxter, with his gentle spirit, Howe, with his penetrating thought, and Jeremy Taylor, with his imagination, rich and glowing as that of

Isaiah himself. Thank God for them, and for the robes they wove for Christ! As I say, we cannot clothe Christ in their garments, but we may learn much from them, and so get power from Christ through them.

Note also that theology is not dead, though particular forms of it have passed away. Every earnest man must have some way of thinking about Christ, and that way is his theology. Perhaps there will be differences; perhaps no two men will think quite alike, or clothe the Saviour in exactly the same garments. It does not matter greatly, I think, for Christ can wear many robes, and be the same Christ still. The great thing is to see to it that our robe of religious thought really touches the person of Christ—that Christ is the centre of our theology. If He be not, no power will be in it, and none can come forth from it, for the real power of the garment is the power of the person who wears it. A theology without Christ may be a very gorgeous robe, but it has no power to give life, because it has no contact with Him who *is* the life. This is the great, the vital difference between differing modes of religious thought. Every one has some sort of theology, whether he acknowledges it or not; even the Atheist has, for his very denial of God is a mode of theological thinking. Some modes of religious thought, however, are dead, powerless, decayed, because they have no living Saviour at the centre of them. Let us understand that no robe can heal but a robe that is worn by Christ. I do not ask you to think of Christ with exactly my thought; I know quite well that He can wear many and widely different garments of human thought; but I do ask you to make Him the centre and the sum of your faith and of your hope. "For there is no other name given under heaven whereby we must be saved." He is "Alpha and Omega, the beginning and the end, the first and the last."

Let us, then, think of different doctrines as of different robes worn by Christ, and let us not quarrel too much with the robe, but try and penetrate through the robe to the Saviour who wears it. Men sometimes hang around Him dry, dusty, threadbare thoughts, so that, seen through them, He seems to have "no form nor comeliness, and there is no beauty that we should desire Him." But do not let the poverty of the robe hide the glory of the wearer. The poorest thing taught and said about Christ will teach and help us if we see Christ in it. And the poorest is not much worse than the best, for who can speak worthily concerning Him? Our words are all

"Too mean to speak His worth,
Too poor to set the Saviour forth."

O Thou who art Thyself the Word, help us to speak of Thee! And do Thou be in our poor speech about Thee, and then it will no longer be poor and mean, but rich with Thy life and tender with Thy love. How blessed is the thought that this poor robe was the vehicle of the healing power of Christ! Thank God, it is not the robe, but the Wearer who is all in all. Even your words and mine are good enough to heal if He is in them; and He has promised that He will be.

When we listen to different theologies and to different preachers, therefore, let us take what suits our case, and let the rest pass. This poor woman took the healing that she needed, and thought no more, I imagine, about the robe through which it came. So let it be with us. Doctrines are many —orthodoxy, heterodoxy, the old school, and the new. But if any man can tell me what brings me nearer to the power and love of Christ, that is what I want. I need pardon for my sin, healing for my bruised and wounded heart, strength for the battle of life. Take that wherever you can get it, and never mind the colour or the texture of the robe through which it comes. When you are starving and a man brings you food you do not criticize the pattern of the dish, you eat the food, and thank God who sent it through him.

The Bible also is a robe of Christ in which His power lives and through which it reaches us. A very wonderful and gorgeous robe it is. There is history and law, poetry and proverb, prophecy and precept—and all are gathered round the central figure of Christ. This is a robe not mean and poor at all, but full of the glow and passion of the splendid East. The Bible is like the bride of the king: " all its garments smell of myrrh, aloes, and cassia, out of the ivory palaces." It is glorious with the gold of Ophir, and resplendent with jewels of the mine. Yet, like everything truly beautiful, it has a noble simplicity in its greatness. There are homely and touching words there, words that reach the hearts of wayfaring men, though they have no distinction of birth and none of the wisdom of the learned. Above all other of the garments of Christ, this one is full of life and power. It fills the intellect, draws the affections to itself, quickens the conscience, strengthens the will. It is not strange that it should be so, for this robe was woven for the Saviour not so much by the skill of man as by the breath of the Divine Spirit itself. We may expect it to be, therefore, as we find it, full of life and power. It is said, and truly, to be " sharper than any two-edged sword." All our means of knowing God are represented in the Bible. There is the history of His doings in the far back ages of the world. There are the lives of the mighty saints in whose souls He dwelt. There are words of warning and of guidance given from His lips. There are the tender pleadings of His love, as of a father with his children. There are words of exceeding great and precious promise. Sorrowing souls come here and find fresh hope and encouragement.

Widowed hearts come and look through its windows to the glad life beyond, where all they loved is waiting for them in purer, nobler forms. Sinful men come and hear the voice of pardoning love and mercy. Broken-hearted penitents come, even Magdalene herself, in her bitter shame and sorrow, and listen to the gracious accents, " Neither do I condemn thee: go and sin no more." Little children come, for there are words of love and blessing for them also, words from the lips of the Divine Son who dwells for ever in the Father's heart. There is life and healing for us all in this robe of the Saviour. Christ's own power is within it, and we may touch and be made whole.

Now I know that some of you may tell me that there are questions raised in the Bible which are not easy to answer, that there are passages of doubtful authorship even, and of uncertain date. I know that there are critics who come to the Bible for science and do not find it; for the robe of Christ, Divine as it is, came to us through human mediums in an age when science was unknown. Shall I therefore discard the Bible and say that it contains nothing for me? My friends, we shall never understand the origin of the Bible till we know what the Bible is; and we shall never know what it is till we use it for its right purpose. Come to the Bible for a revelation of God; see God manifest in Jesus Christ at its centre—all that goes before pointing forward, and all that comes

after pointing back to the central figure of Christ,
and you will know what it means. The decisive
evidence that the sword of the Spirit is of celestial
temper, is in its power to cut down our sins,
and to protect us from our spiritual foes. The
Christ whom we need is here, and here He shall
be lifted up until He draws all men unto Himself.

But again, the Church of Christ is one of the
garments in which He dwells, and through which His
healing virtue flows. And by the Church of Christ
I do not mean the Roman Church, or the Anglican,
the Presbyterian, or the Congregational. These
are sections of the Church more or less good and
perfect ; but the Church itself is greater than any,
because it includes them all. No sect can say, in
an exclusive sense, " The people of the Lord are
we "; none, at all events, can say so without
egregious arrogance. Christ dwells in His whole
Church, not in a part of it only, and His Church
consists of all holy men everywhere. When I say
that Christ dwells in His Church, I mean that He
dwells in all who love His name in every age and
in every country. His Church is " a great multi-
tude of every kindred, and nation, and people, and
tongue." It has spoken many languages and
worshipped in many forms. Sometimes it has
gathered in a vast cathedral, where pealing anthems
soared to its fretted roof, and " the dim religious
light " came mellowed through " storied windows

richly dight." Sometimes in a scantily-furnished
room with no ornaments save those of the meek
and quiet spirits who bowed and worshipped there.
" For neither in Jerusalem nor at Mount Gerizim
do men worship the Father ; but the true worshippers worship Him in spirit and in truth."
Wherever there are holy souls there is a true house
of God. And this pure, spiritual Church Christ
wears as a garment, and through it He communi-
cates His healing power to men. I do not say that
all sections of the Church are equally good and
wise. I do not think so. For reasons that seem
to me conclusive I can worship best with a simple
ritual. I need no priest save Christ Himself. But
the important fact is that we can find life in any
church if we go there seeking the right thing—the
healing power of Christ. Men and women, let us
take care what we seek. If we seek a gorgeous ritual
we can easily obtain it, but it will not necessarily en-
lighten our minds and purify our hearts. If we seek
a Scriptural form of church government or service,
we may discover that, and it may turn out to be as
perfectly destitute of living power as a beautiful
corpse. But if we touch any of the many fringes
of His garment seeking His life-giving energy,
Christ Himself will meet us and speak to us as He
did to this poor suppliant at His feet. It matters
less *to* which church we go, than *for what* we go.
Fix your gaze, then, on the central figure, Jesus
Christ Himself ; press through the crowd until you

feel His touch and hear His voice, and He will make you whole.

But mark, if Christ is in His Church it is perilous for you and me to seek to do without the Church. Some say that they will stand alone in religion. But this is not the plan of God for us. We cannot live alone in anything, and least of all in religion; for religion is especially social. Faith is redoubled when we share it with others; so are hope, love, joy, peace. Your penitence and trust kindle mine; my prayer and praise are wings to yours. These Divine things grow by sharing them; only selfishness would seek their exclusive appropriation. Touch this robe of Christ if you would understand the blessedness of the communion of saints—the strength and solace that comes out of union with each other in Him who is the Head.

But I must point out, in a word or two, that *we* have robes as well as Christ, and that in a lesser degree, of course, power and energy flow from these also. Scripture uses the idea of garments constantly as a figure for character. There is a priestly and a kingly robe. Joseph had a coat of many colours, as though to express the fact that he was the son of many affections. And we hear of the "white linen, which is the righteousness of the saints," of "robes washed and made white in the blood of the Lamb." The life of Christ, which gives us the white robe, not only takes away the stain of sin, it fills the purified soul with its own Divine essence.

Now, as our robes are our characters, there is an influence going forth from them as there was from the robe of Christ. First of all, then, we must see that we obtain our white raiment, our robe of righteousness, from the Saviour. He can clothe even the little child with His purity and loveliness. He can add dignity and strength to the young man as he steps into the arena of life. He can glorify the wedding garment of the bride with sweetness and modesty. He can add lustre to the robe of honour as it is gathered round the limbs of the brave warrior in the battle of life. And when the hoary head is a crown of glory, He can beautify their declining days with the saintly garments of holiness and peace. Our perpetual characters, beloved, are the robes in which we shall be clad when we appear before God. May He grant them to have been washed and made white by Christ Himself, that we may not be ashamed before Him, at His coming.

VI.

CHARACTER AND DESTINY.

¹ "But the Lord said unto Samuel, Look not on his countenance, or on the height of his stature, . . . for the Lord
seeth not as man seeth ; for man looketh on the outward
appearance, but the Lord looketh on the heart."—1 SAM.
xvi. 7.

IT was a crisis in the history of the nation. Saul
had forfeited the favour of God. He had only
now to decline to the end of his reign, dishonoured
and rejected. Samuel had done with him. And
Samuel was come to Bethlehem to choose among
the sons of Jesse he who should be king after Saul.
I suppose the choice was made while Saul was still
alive, that the king-elect might prepare for his
high destiny. It is not good for us to change our
position or our work too suddenly. We need
thought, deliberation, the adjustment of ourselves
to our new duties. It was well that he who was to
be king should prepare himself for what was
before him. It was well that he should nourish
his heart in kingly thought, swathe his spirit in
true royalty and magnanimity.

When the sons of Jesse came before Samuel, he looked at them with eyes full of scrutiny. First came Eliab; tall, strong, of manly bearing, of frank and noble countenance. " Surely," he said to himself, " this is the man whom the Lord hath chosen." But then came a whisper, a rush of inspired thought into his heart, " Take care, look not on his countenance, nor on the height of his stature, for the Lord seeth not as man seeth, for man looketh on the outward appearance, but the Lord looketh on the heart." The question is whether the hidden springs of character are there, and whether they are healthy and operative. There is a power that is only material. Fair, but perishable, it passes away. There is another kind of power, one with the springs of man's essential life. It belongs to his heart—to the innermost, secret place of his thinking and feeling. Eliab may be captivating. In his own way he may be noble and strong; but the strength that grows with years, and can adapt itself to every need, is not in him. You must go to David for that. David, as we shall see presently, is the man who, though far enough from perfect, yet for this particular business of kingship is " after God's own heart." David is the born king.

Now this is the great principle of the text—that in all things God looks not at appearances, but on realities. When He deals with us, or we with Him, it must be on a basis of absolute truth and

fact. He is not, cannot be, deceived; and, on His
part, He never deceives. "All things are naked
and opened to the eyes of Him with whom we have
to do." We ought to be glad of this. Some
people shrink away from the thought of God
because they know that He is looking them
through and through. What they mean by it I
do not know. Do they desire to be treated in a
manner inappropriate to their true condition? If
you were in danger of death or loss, would you
wish the friend on whom you leaned to act as
though you were well or secure? I think you
know better. You know the only way to deal with
disease is to face it; the only way to avoid danger
is to know it, and guard against it. That is God's
way. He looketh at the heart; the heart of men,
and the heart—the innermost reality—of things
too. He does so, for example, with reference to
our vocation in life. There are different estimates
of fitness for work that needs to be done. It was
so in the case we are considering. The people were
about to need a leader. They had to find one.
Samuel was as wise a man as any to whom they
could entrust the choice, no doubt; and yet Samuel
was near to making a great mistake. Even he
was almost carried away by the outward appearance of Eliab. There, he thought, was surely the
warrior king. But no. Courage may go with
strength, indeed, but more than courage and
strength are needed in a leader of men. Insight,

sympathy, administrative power, skill, self-control, a widely inclusive nature, are needed as much, or even more, than mere physical strength. The real hero is little David there. He had "nourished a youth sublime," as he led his sheep by the green pastures and still waters of his native land, or looked up into the starry skies as he watched his flock by night. Latent in his character were the seeds, the first principles, from which his splendid reign was evolved. For of all the leaders the Hebrew people ever had David was, by emphasis, the king.

Now, I desire that you and I should apply this principle of the text to our own lives. Most people whom I meet are dissatisfied with life. It does not yield them what they expected. If they had their time to come over again they would do differently and bring about quite other, and more satisfactory, results. Generally people are not as prominent or as successful as they think they deserve to be ; others more fortunate and less worthy are preferred before them. I have no doubt many thought so in Israel. "David, indeed ! who is he that he should rule us ? Why, I could toss him on the point of my spear !" says a stalwart warrior. "Look at this beardless youth," exclaims a grave counsellor ; "they are passing by the wise and experienced, and choosing a lad who knows nothing but what he has learnt in the sheep-fold ! "

But Samuel had made the God-directed choice. He who seeth not as man seeth had singled out the true king.

Of course I do not mean that every man is actually in the position for which he is most fitted. But I do mean that our own choice, and that of other people's for us, is often superficial and untrue. Let us learn a lesson from the shepherd-boy. Did he go about complaining that he was a neglected genius, with his merits all unrecognized? No. He kept his sheep. He was put to do that, and he did it. He kept his sheep so well that he learnt to keep the flock of God. Then, in due time, he was chosen for the office for which he was fitted. God put him into his right place.

Now I daresay some of us are dreadfully unappreciated. The world is governed with very little wisdom. And if people only knew what we deserved, they would give us prominent office, and perhaps twenty thousand a year! But, you see, they do not know. God, however, knows the fact, and the whole fact. Perhaps He sees that we are better for the present on the hillside than on the throne. If so, let us stay feeding our Father's flocks till He anoints us to something else. And let us learn that the way to better things is earnest work and loving contentment with the lot He gives.

And suppose even that we are right in our estimate of ourselves. Suppose that man *has* looked on the outward appearance, and has put over our heads a less worthy person, a foolish man, a knave, or a poor incompetent sham. Well, God knows that too. It might have been that David tended sheep all his life, and that Saul was succeeded by a man as insane as himself. But would not God have known it? Would not God have cared for it? Would not He have thought more of the shepherd singing his lovely psalms under the Syrian skies than of the poor nonentity reigning at Jerusalem? It is not *where* we are, but *what* we are, that is of real and permanent consequence. All the glitter of wealth, all the splendour of office, all that makes the outward appearance, imposes only upon man ; God looketh on the heart.

The principle of our text holds also with reference to our usefulness. What good are we doing in the world? Men think they can easily answer that question. They take the first and most obvious estimate. How much noise are we making? How many people are hearing of us? What figure do we present in the church or among the societies that are organized for special forms of benevolence? I daresay if Eliab had been compared with David, the public verdict would have gone almost entirely for Eliab. There was not much that men could see, that they could count or weigh or measure in the modest employment of David. He was keeping a few sheep, that was all. But *was* it all? Verily, no. The eye of God saw another and a

greater work. He was building up a kingly character. He was feeding his spirit in secret, and
doing the duty nearest to him. In that way,
though there was little outward show, the *man* was
developing into fitness for the greater work which
God was preparing for him.

There is nothing that we more need to recon-
sider than our standard of usefulness in God's
kingdom. Thousands of hearts are made sad
whom the Lord has not made sad by our shallow,
foolish judgments. In the church we are too apt
to judge men's piety by the sound they make, especially in the way of fault-finding. To criticize the
goodness of others is a short and easy method of
proclaiming the superior quality of our own.
Look suspiciously upon any one who attempts
fresh means of advancing the cause of God ; shake
your head at any who are desirous of getting out
of ruts ; or take up some doctrinal fad, about the
second advent, or the discovery of the ten tribes,
and though you may be somewhat of a bore, you
will doubtless gain the reputation of being deeply
pious. But oh, friends, how easy is all that !
And how difficult it is to do the will of God in your
daily duty, and to breathe around you the gentle
and tender spirit of Jesus! Verily, man seeth not
as God seeth. Man looketh on the outward appearance, but God looketh on the heart.

Take comfort, then, you who are trying quietly
to help others and to keep yourself in the love of

God. Take comfort, you who are doing *real* work, whether in the church or out of it. Take comfort, you who in any way are striving to ennoble your own lives and those of others. If you are too busy doing good to be harsh or censorious to other people, so much the better for you. If your heart is so warm with the love of Christ that it finds or makes warmth in the hearts of those around, you have cause to rejoice. You will find love and peace and joy in thus working for God.

Toiling men, who are honest and true, and who fight against your sins and doubts, when it seems as though God had forgotten you, and the clouds of failure and disappointment shut out the sunlight of faith and hope, God knows all about it. Fight on, and trust. The time is coming when you will conquer. He will bring out your righteousness as the light, and your "equity" as the noonday. Meanwhile, let the thought that God *does* know—that while men are looking at the appearance, He is looking into your heart—be your strength and hope. It is possible, nay easy, to bear being overlooked by men, if we have His "Well done, good and faithful servant!" ringing in our hearts.

Anxious, thoughtful women, bearing in your hearts brothers, husbands, children, you may not make much figure in the world. But take comfort. There is not a sigh you breathe, a tear you shed, or a prayer you utter, that is not marked by

God. Perhaps, little as you think it, you are doing
the greatest work for Him. And be sure that you
are not left to do it alone. Little notice you may
obtain from any whom the world calls great; but
remember that He who looketh on the heart looks
specially on the anxious, loving, bleeding, sometimes almost breaking, woman's heart.

As to moral and religious conduct too, the principle of our text is true. How superficially we
judge ! We separate the world into good and bad,
but we scarcely see an inch deep into the reality
of character. When the light of God shines on
men, at what we call the judgment-day, many
people will be astonished at the grouping of character they will see. If there is any truth in the
words of Christ, our estimates will be as nearly as
possible reversed. We make scandalous sins—the
sins of the poor, weak flesh, which become visible
and notorious—the worst form of sin. Christ
makes the sins of the spirit—pride, vainglory, the
conceit of special righteousness, the sanctimonious
separation of ourselves from others—these and the
like, Christ makes the worst. No wonder. Every
man knows the publicans and sinners, and the
shame of poor Perdita. They scandalize us all,
and we draw away our immaculate skirts as we
pass by. But a man may be full of malignity
and hatred, and no one know it but God. Did it
ever occur to you that it is not wise to judge other
men ? Nay, did you ever happen to feel thankful

that you do not need to judge? We know sometimes what is done, but do we know what is resisted? We see the sin, but do we see the bitter, heartbroken repentance? "O God," we may well cry, "I thank Thee that *Thou* art my judge, and not man. I thank Thee that Thou who knowest my sin, knowest also how I abhor myself, and take thankful refuge in Thy dear love in Christ."

Some people think of the words of my text with terror. To me they are full of joy and hope. "The Lord seeth not as man seeth . . . the Lord looketh on the heart." They read like the words of Jesus Himself; they are a gospel to all poor, struggling souls. It is not the stately Pharisee, with his broad phylactery and his flowing robe that is accepted. No, it is nothing that appeals to the eyes of men. But if there is a spirit here that is tired of sin and thirsty for God, God looks on such an one with love and favour. If there is one broken heart, sick and sore with past transgression, God in Christ is saying, "Come unto Me, and I will give you rest." If there is a bright young soul, who, having felt the beauty of holiness, is stirred with a holy ambition to reach the true eternal life, God smiles upon that soul, and says, through the lips of His own Son, "Blessed are they that hunger and thirst after righteousness, for they shall be filled." If there is one who has looked at Christ till he has seen Him to be the Divine-human Saviour—"the chiefest among ten thousand, and

11

the altogether lovely "—oh, beloved, the Lord looketh upon *thee.* Yes, and if there is one here who is hard and cold, and yet has an indefinite regret at his own hardness, come, let Him look upon *thy* heart too. His look of love will melt it; His poured-out life will flow over and into your indifference; His power shall set you free. For us all there is moral health and spiritual renewal in the blessed fact that He is looking upon our hearts. May we each one cry, "Search me, O God, and know my heart; try me, and know my thoughts, and see if there be any evil way in me, and lead me in the way everlasting."

VII.

WATER FROM BETHLEHEM.

"And David longed, and said, Oh that one would give me water to drink of the well of Bethlehem, which is by the gate! And the three brake through the host of the Philistines, and drew water out of the well of Bethlehem, that was by the gate, and took it, and brought it to David: but David would not drink thereof, but poured it out unto the Lord, and said, My God forbid it me, that I should do this: shall I drink the blood of these men that have put their lives in jeopardy? for with the jeopardy of their lives they brought it."—1 CHRON. xi. 17-19.

THIS is one of the jewels of history. It is worth while to read a book, and a dry book too, to get at a fact so heroic and noble. It is a beautiful fragment, glittering with moral splendour, embedded like a precious stone in the tamer, poorer matter which surrounds it. Of the three men spoken of here, we do not, it is true, know much; their very names are matters of guess-work. And yet in another sense we know a great deal of them. For names and dates, and all other outward relations of history, are of use only as they throw light

on the characters of man and nations, on the
inward impulses from which their actions flow.
And this one act seems to open a rift by which we
see into the very souls of those by whom it could
be done. There is a voice within us, too, which
responds and rejoices in the story of their nobleness. We are the richer for the knowledge of what
they did. Thousands of years have not dimmed
the value of their heroism.

There is a greatness, too, about David's conduct,
which accounts for our love for him. For we do
love David. We sometimes, no doubt, wonder at
our fondness. He was a man very far from perfect.
The unbelievers of all ages have " held him dang-
ling at arm's length in scorn." " This is the man
after God's own heart ! " they say. Yes, even so.
Not immaculate, not always wise or good, but
one who knew how to be sorry for his sin ; for he
loved much, and to whom much was therefore forgiven. David sinned indeed, but he repented as
greatly as he sinned. If his passions were great,
and his fall deep and terrible, his love and his
repentance were vast too. "Passions that are
great, passions moving in a vast orbit, and trans-
cending little regards, are always," De Quincey
tells us, " the signs of a noble mind." There is
assuredly that nobleness, that largeness of mind,
about David. We cannot resist it. It lifts us up
and carries us away. We have to love him
whether we will or no.

The fact before us is grand. Let us look at it briefly, and see what it says to us.

We see that we may be generous in receiving as well as in giving. Here there was a noble generosity from both points of view. For what is generosity? It is nobility, largeness of nature. The root syllable "gen" tells us this, for it is connected with the words "generate" and "generation." So that a generous man is a man belonging to a generation worth thinking about and worth belonging to. How did these heroes give, and how did David receive, this precious gift? "And David longed and said, Oh that one would give me water to drink of the well of Bethlehem, which is by the gate!" The fighting had been fierce under the glowing Eastern sky. The man's burning thirst craved assuagement. And then there flashed into his mind the remembrance of the old well in the old Bethlehem days. How often in the parching summer heat he had drunk from its cool, refreshing spring. Never was anything so delicious, so life-restoring. We all know something of the feeling which makes what we have enjoyed in youth so much sweeter and keener and more vivid to our recollection than anything that later years can bring. Perhaps some who are listening to me now can go back in thought to some such memory, "when all the world was young." The old home, the old garden, the old childish haunts, may be commonplace enough to others, but for you they are fraught with tenderest suggestions. "The touch of the vanished hand" is there, and "the sound of a voice that is still."

"And the three brake through the host of the Philistines, and drew water out of the well of Bethlehem, that was by the gate, and took it, and brought it to David: but David would not drink thereof, and poured it out unto the Lord, and said, My God forbid it me, that I should do this: shall I drink the blood of these men that have put their lives in jeopardy? for with the jeopardy of their lives they brought it." Our hearts glow within us as we read the story. "Heroes all!" we say. It is a problem I could not solve, whether it is greater to inspire such love, or to feel it. Only a hero, a truly great soul could inspire it. But then, only heroes could feel it. How many men would have done such a deed to-day? Many, do you say? I hope so. But as compared with the great mass they would be a minority; aye, and a small minority too. You could not pour a love like that into cold, calculating hearts. The "frozen hearts and hasting feet" of the great world are incapable of feeling it. There is a class of animals, you know, who do not appreciate pearls; and there are classes of men who move in an orbit so small, so mean, and so selfish, that nothing could move them to generosity.

But David was not behind his heroes in his mode of receiving the gift. To him the material gift—

the bright, sparkling water of his beloved spring—
faded away and was dissolved in the generosity of
the givers. He saw a spiritual revelation gathered
round it. He saw all the peril to which they had
been put, and the love which lay behind the peril.
It was sacred, all that. It was worthy of the best
and highest in the universe. "My God," he cries,
"shall I drink the blood of these men that have
put their lives in jeopardy? for with their lives
they brought it." And he poured it out before the
Lord.

That, now, is a great gift greatly received; and
it is full of instruction for us, for we are also
givers and receivers. We are, whether we will or
no. It is one of the truths that the science of our
day has taught us that we are actually *made* by
what we receive from former generations and from
other people. We, who think ourselves so independent, are in large part the creation of the people
and circumstances around us, and of an indefinite
past; every faculty, every power, every form of
our activity is rooted and grounded in what others
have thought and felt and done. If I am wise
and good I owe it largely to the wisdom and goodness of some who were wise and good who have
gone before, and are now lying in their quiet
graves, and of others who taught me in my youth,
and surrounded me with purity as an atmosphere.
We, who receive so much, what are we giving to
those around us, and to those who will come after

us? And *how* are we giving? Are we giving as
these men did, with eager generosity, or are we
giving with a tight fist and with a tighter heart?
Are we seeking that all that goes out from us—
thought, words, actions—the thousand minute influences that cannot be reduced to a class or receive
a name—shall only tend to purify and elevate?
Do we feel that we cannot live to ourselves, and
ought not? Have we discovered that the fact that
we are "members one of another" reaches far
deeper into the truth of things than the little
spark of self-consciousness which we call "me,"
and of which we think so much? Of course much
of our influence is unconscious. Men are receiving
from us when we do not know it, nor they either.
But even the unconscious part of our giving
is largely within our control, for it takes its
tone, its colouring, its temperature, so to speak,
from what we think and feel in our habitual state of
mind. *Be* good, *i.e.*, think and feel according to
goodness, and you can no more help *doing* good
than the sun can help shining, because its very
being is light and heat. So also as to what we
give consciously. It may, if we will, grow to be
our chief joy. To these men it was a far greater
joy than receiving. So it will be with us when we
are full of love. Then it will matter very little
what we give. We may give a cup of water to the
thirsty, a flower to one who loves it, and longs for
it, some hidden office of love to a lonely and deso-

late heart. The same is true of receiving. There is an ungenerous way of receiving, as well as of giving. Stingy givers are bad enough; they lower the pulse of life, they degrade the energy of generous feeling. But they are not half so bad as ungenerous receivers. I have known them, have not you? Men who grasp all favours as their due—who, as one has said, more emphatically than elegantly, "receive their mercies with a grunt." Some even throw back acts of love and think nothing of the bitter pain they inflict. There are wives in our quiet homes to-day whose hearts are half-broken by such slights as these. Some pleasant surprise planned for their husband is received with cool indifference, or with an unappreciative frown. Or is it never the husband who is so treated? Do, I pray you, think of it—the pain of love thrown back upon itself. How many faithful eyes ache for a kind glance? how many ears listen in vain for a loving word?

And is not the same principle true of the highest things? We are doers of service, you and I. We do service to our Lord and Master, Jesus Christ. How? With a loyalty and love like theirs who put their lives in jeopardy for their Captain and King? David is not the only sovereign who has been splendidly served. Our own Queen Elizabeth was. She was surrounded by such men as Raleigh, and Spenser, Bacon, and Drake. They carried their lives in their hands for her honour, and found a

rich reward in her smile of approbation. Cromwell
was so served. His presence was an inspiration,
his word of command a trumpet-note of energy.
Even Napoleon, a smaller and less worthy hero,
knew how to make himself beloved and obeyed.
And is not Christ worthy of our loyalty—yea, of
our utmost heroism? For what is the love of
Christ and the service of Christ but the love and
service of all goodness and chivalry, truth and
honour? He asks no strictly personal service.
He receives no crown or robe or costly offering at
our hands. He clothes Himself with the everlasting laws of purity and mercy and truth, and
tells us to embody our loyalty by fulfilling these.
Serve Him faithfully, you who are called by His
name. For you He has more than risked—He has
laid down, His precious life. He has brought us,
not a cup of cold water, but the very health and
life of our souls. How shall we receive the gift?
Shall we take it as the pleasant song of a tuneful
voice, and then let it die into forgetfulness? Or
shall we pour out our redeemed souls, as David
poured out the blood-bought water, to spend and
be spent for Him?

> " Our Master all the work hath done,
>   He asks of us to-day :
> Sharing His service, every one
>   Share too His Sonship may :
> Lord, I would serve, and be a son ;
>   Dismiss me not, I pray."

One more lesson in closing. We often do the most useful things when we are not thinking at all of usefulness. David poured out this water *to the Lord*. He was not thinking of use, I suppose, in any way. It was with him as with the woman who broke the alabaster box of ointment and poured it over the Saviour's feet. The Pharisees were shocked at the waste. Was it not valuable? Could it not have been sold, and the money have been given to the poor? Even to use it for herself, they thought, would have been more rational than simply to pour it away. But David and the woman were right, and their critics altogether wrong. There are uses quite beyond what we mean by use. Love must manifest itself; and the very manifestation is the largest and the truest good. And if you join the Pharisees, and cry "What waste!" I answer, "No, I think not." For waste is a relative idea: what is wasted for one purpose may be saved for another. This act of David's was wasteful as to the quenching of his thirst. But it did better even for David than in giving him that temporary refreshment. It elevated his whole spiritual nature. It brought him nearer to the God to whom the precious gift was consecrated. He who knew what it was to be thirsty for God, who had cried, "As the hart panteth after the waterbrooks, so panteth my soul after Thee, O God," was refreshed with a draught of spiritual renewal. The water, had he drunk it, would have left him to thirst again; but offered in sacrifice to God it was in him "as a well of water, springing up unto everlasting life." The same is true of whatever tends to ennoble the spiritual nature, to approximate us, in other words, to "the likeness of Christ." "Does it pay?" you ask. No, it does not pay, as the world counts payment. You cannot buy love at so much a pound, nor bargain for faith and nobleness by the yard. Yet in a deeper, truer sense, these things do pay. For they are the very treasures which have no relation to time and space; precious to God; watched over by Him, "where neither moth nor rust doth corrupt, and where thieves do not break through and steal."

For our best things belong to God. Because this water was precious as the lives of men, *therefore* David offered it to God. It is not the parings of our time, the refuse of our thought, the overplus of our profits, that must be set apart to Him; it is all in our lives which is best and noblest. For God accepts our sacrifices and values them in proportion as they make us better. A purer faith, hands quicker unto good, a ripening, mellowing love, a peace that deepens till it "passeth all understanding"—this is the purpose of our sacrifices, and the fulfilment of our Father's Divine intention. Beloved, "this is the will of God concerning you."

VIII.

THE VARIATION OF STRENGTH.

"But they that wait on the Lord shall renew their strength; they shall mount up with wings as eagles; they shall run, and not be weary; they shall walk and not faint."—Isa. xl. 31.

"EVEN the youths shall faint and be weary, and the young men shall utterly fall." So it was in that old world in which the prophet lived. If he had lived to-day what would he have said? Life was difficult, complicated, anxious, even then. It required courage to face it rightly, for it was full of burden and sorrow. Youths in the spring-tide of energy, young men in the splendour of opening faculty, felt its heavy weight, so that they lay weary and broken by the wayside. I suppose it has been so ever since. We are proud to look back with longing eyes, and to fancy that the times past were better than these. We speak of the leisure and the wisdom of the days that are gone. But there has, I think, been no time at which the majority of men have not found it hard to live, at

which the wise and the leisurely have not been few
and far between. I am disposed to think that
" this time is equal to all time that's past." Pressed
though we are on every side, we have immense
compensations. Life is fuller and larger when we
regard the majority of mankind, and I do not know
that it is much more laborious ; at all events,
the labour is not so servile and degrading.
There is indeed a " bitter cry " of toil and want,
which let us never forget. But there is a large
heart in men to set over against it, and a consciousness of solidarity — of our interest in one
another—such as the world has never before seen.
The youth to-day is born to higher knowledge and
to wider sympathy. The young man, if he fall, is
more likely than of old to be lifted with tenderness
and set on his feet again. Indeed it must be so,
for we live in the nineteenth century after Christ,
and Christ has fulfilled His own promise. If He
has gone away, He has also come again. And the
wider thought of man which we entertain, as well
as our truer care for our fellows, is the manifestation, the very pulse-beat, of His presence.

But what was the remedy for the weariness that
grows out of the battle of life ? It was the consciousness of the spiritual world. " They that wait
on the Lord shall renew their strength." So that
they shall have no fatal or final discouragement.
Their consciousness of God shall save them, and
that in various ways. By the presence and power

of God they shall renew their strength, when otherwise they would "faint," or even "utterly fall." A great gift is that—to renew our *strength*. We do not see always that it is our fundamental need. We cry for *rest*. There are even times when we would gladly lay down life itself and sleep in our quiet graves. But we mistake our real need. It is not inactivity. Still less is it death. It is a fresh quickening, a new inspiration of life. The teacher who has sung for us more wisdom than almost any other of our time, says that—

> "'Tis life of which our veins are scant,
> More life, and fuller that we want."

See, then, how this new strength shows itself.

In a generous enthusiasm. "They shall mount up with wings as eagles." The figure is beautiful. We are told, indeed, that it is not our British eagle which is the bird here meant, but the large white-headed vulture which inhabited the mountain ranges and lofty crags of Palestine. But both birds have this quality in common: they lift up their vast pinions, beating the air with their powerful wings as they leave their nests and ascend the skies; they have a wheeling, spiral method of flight, rising in the air to lofty mountain elevations, from whence they may survey the plains beneath.

So also they that wait upon the Lord. They mount up into the clear sky, they lift up pinions

that will enable them to mount; and then they
get the far-extended vision of Divine as well as
human things.   They see man and God in their
essential character and true relations.   They gaze
on the sun of spiritual truth undaunted, and
gloriously receptive of all His light and warmth.
The eagle—

> " Clasps the crag with hookèd hands,
>   Close to the sun' n lonely lands."

It is great and glorious.   But notice, carefully,
that the strength that mounts up into the heights
of comprehensive vision and enraptured feeling,
though noble, is not the *noblest* form of power.
Our text is cumulative—it goes from great to greater.
It is great to " mount up with wings as eagles ";
it is greater still to " run and not be weary "; it is
greatest of all to " walk and not faint."   At
first sight it may not seem so, but you will soon see
that it is.   For what does this lofty flight mean ?
It means the new vision of the world and life, and
of the character of God, with which we start on our
onward journey, after our strength has been
renewed by waiting on the Lord.   There are such
moments in most men's lives.   We call for help,
we look at the past, we ponder the great truths
that are incarnate in the life of Christ.   Suddenly the day dawns and the shadows flee away.
All our life to its inmost recesses seems lighted up;

its mystery becomes intelligible. We see the hand of God, and hear the tones of His tender love where we never thought to find them. Full of responsive gratitude and joy our soul rises towards heaven. For a little while, at least, " We see as we are seen, and know as we are known." Thank God for it all. It is life, hope, inspiration. Nay, it is necessary sometimes, if we are to be saved from actual death. It must be with us, as with others, " See God and live." But the vision is not all we need. Most of our life is not, and cannot, be spent in the rapture of the third heaven. Even Christ had to come down again from the mount of transfiguration, and so must we. The face of Moses shone as he came from his communion with God, but when he took the veil away, it had become like the face of another man. Make no mistake, my friends; the eagle's wing is not the highest gift; the sight of the sun is only granted as an inspiration for something nobler still. As Christ on the cross is really greater than Christ on the mount, so the man who is following Him in sorrow and toil is doing more than the most ecstatic visionary to purify his own soul and to realize the kingdom of God. God give you the eagle's wing—God grant you to be caught up in spirit to heaven, and to hear words which it is not possible for man to utter; but that should only brace your energies for work, and prepare you to do and dare mighty things amongst sinning and suffering men.

12

Here is a swift obedience. "They shall run and not be weary." The idea of running suggests a perfect willingness, as well as an immediate reduction of command to practice. This comes to us also by waiting on the Lord; it comes through the lofty visions which are given by the eagle's wing. Truth lies at the bottom of all healthy activity, and activity is admirable just in proportion as the truth from which it springs is profound and elevating. For the highest truths concern not our thoughts alone, but all our powers—emotional and voluntary, as well as intellectual. They seize and transfigure our entire being. They become irresistible impulse as well as material for reflection. A man may be mainly a thinker, but if his thought becomes part of his life it kindles his activities to a blaze. And this is what the world and the Church of to-day are both needing: men who know how to bring speculation and insight into the practical aspects of the great problems that meet us on every side. It is *applied* knowledge for which the world is thirsting. The running foot that carries help and love to the ignorant and vicious; the swift thought that understands by a flash of intuition what is to be *done;* the living insight that discerns the connection between great thoughts and those common duties in which they are embodied and expressed ;— these are what we need. For never forget that the true idea of practical Christianity is this—" great thoughts underlying small duties." Is not this the character of Christ? Was not all the light and love of eternity in the very smallest of His deeds? The tears by the grave of Lazarus, the tender care over young children, the delicate considerateness that He showed for every individual soul He met,—are they not that blessed "running without weariness," which is more than the noblest vision of truth, although sustained and guided by its inspiration?

Here is a persevering toil. "They shall walk and not faint." Walking differs from running in that it is a slower form of movement and springs from a less impulsive energy. When we are full of the irrepressible powers of a rejoicing life we are likely to run. When we have a long journey to take, and are compelled to measure our strength against the toil, walking suits us better. The text implies that it is this kind of walking of which the writer thinks—the weary plodding along an almost endless road, which tests the persistence of every nerve and muscle of the body. That is a more difficult achievement than to mount on the strong wings of the eagle, or to run along the pathway of glad, rejoicing impulse. It is not in the battle, amid the sharp notes of the trumpet, the inspiring commands of the captain, and the shouting of a thousand voices, that the horse's strength is tried; it is in the long, monotonous tread on the dusty high-road. The same principle holds true in the spiritual life. The real trial of character is in the weariness of daily duty, and especially in those actions that seem so small and unimportant as to make us wonder whether they are worthy to be called duties at all. We find our true test, not on the mountain-top of spiritual vision, not even when with willing feet we run on some special errand of love or heroic achievement, but when we do our little humble duties as "to-morrow, and to-morrow, and to-morrow, creeps on its weary pace from day to day." I doubt whether, when all is seen, the most illustrious martyrs will prove to be those who came even out of the "great tribulation" of Nero's persecution,—those whose life-blood hissed on the cruel flame, or whose living bones were crunched in the jaws of the lion. Their names are dear to us, and we raise the "costly tomb and marble cenotaph" to their memories; but perhaps those eyes that see everywhere perceive still more heroism in the daily toil of some faithful husband and loving father, who for long years has worked with a body racked by disease and mind distracted by nervous tremor, to keep his humble home together, to comfort his wife, to educate his children, and to do his quiet duty to man and to God. Or the crown of honour may be placed still more conspicuously on the brows of some unknown wife and mother, who has maintained her home in the solitude of an unloved heart, for the sake of a drunken husband, and children too young to appreciate the sacrifices by which they are reared. I wish I could carry a word of consolation to you, whoever you may be, who walk the weary path of life, and, for the sake of God and Christ, do not faint. Young man, in some unlovely business house, in this great London, God sees you as you spend lonely hours and think with tears you will not shed of your home far away. He waits to be mother and father, sister and brother to you. If you keep yourself pure, and quietly do the duty to which He calls you, it is not you that do it, but Christ who dwelleth in you. That "patient continuance in well doing," which now looks so monotonous, and seems so un-noticed, is precious in the sight of God—is, indeed, the prelude to "glory, honour, immortality, eternal life"! Young woman, sitting alone in your attic room, and wondering whether you will ever again have about you the warmth and glow of your beloved home, what you need is a vision of your Saviour; and you, too, shall do more than mount on eagle's wings—you shall walk the lonely road without fainting, for you shall be strong in the Lord and in the power of His life. Believe me, it is not for naught that you are called to endure the cross. It is these unseen and unnoticed trials that develop and ennoble character. They not only test, but make perfect, the life of Christ in the soul. They may be preparing for you various successes *here*, and they are certainly preparing you for the larger, prouder life beyond.

And so of us all. Our daily pain, our constant burden, that dull ache which we conceal beneath our smile of welcome to our friends, our failing strength, our disappointed hope, are the means of a development into the true life that never passes away. To bear them, and to do in loving acceptance the duties they involve, is our witness, our martyrdom for Christ. Not a pang is lost, not an effort or a sigh, but enters into that vast whole, which is the result of God's completed plan.

IX

A SHINING FACE.

"And when Aaron and all the children of Israel saw Moses, behold, the skin of his face shone; and they were afraid to come nigh him."—Exod. xxxiv. 30.

I IMAGINE it was a beautiful sight, this shining face of Moses. He was a man, as we must believe, of noble and commanding presence. When he was a child his mother saw that he was very beautiful—"beautiful to God," as the expressive Hebrew has it. Mothers are not always impartial judges; but in this case, no doubt, she was right. In our text we have the people, and even Aaron, overpowered at the majesty of his presence. To the natural beauty of the man had been added a spiritual glory, so bright that they could scarcely bear its radiance. Whence came the shining of Moses' face, and what did it mean? Why did the people stand in awe of him? There are several answers. One is that it was a miracle, and that we had better not ask any questions about it. Another answer is an old sceptical one—that Moses'

face did not shine at all, but that he pretended
it shone, in order to make an impression on the
people and gain currency for his laws. But this
will not satisfy me ; for it amounts to saying that
this man, who gave the Jews a code of laws that
has lived for thousands of years, was a poor im-
postor, who maintained his authority by cheating.
But great kings, great lawgivers, great men, are
not impostors.   They leave imposture to people
who have nothing better to offer ; they do not need
it themselves.   Another view is that the face of
Moses was expressive of excitement and exaltation,
so that it seemed to shine—as we speak of a face
blazing with anger or blushing with shame.   This
is nearer the mark, yet not quite all the truth
either.   The truth is shared, I think, between this
view and the opinion that the shining of Moses'
face was a miracle.

For what is a miracle ? Something wonderful or
unusual done by God.   But is a miracle, therefore,
unnatural ?   Is it *contrary* to the laws of nature ?
Is it out of all relation to everything we know,
so that we cannot at all understand it ?   Christ's
wonderful cures were miracles because they were
effected quickly and at once, and we therefore seem
to *see* the power of God in them.   But is not the
power of God present when a wise and loving
physician cures us ?   Does he not do it by the
very same power which dwelt without measure in
Christ ?   It seems to me that miracles are not so

much violations of the laws of nature as these very laws carried up to a nobler and loftier degree. The physician works by what means? By knowledge and by love. And Christ wrought by the same means, only by an infinitely higher knowledge and an infinitely deeper love.

Now, apply this to the shining of Moses' face. Moses had been on the mount. He had been there to commune with God — to come into direct contact with His mind and will. Alone there, with the silence of the desert around him, and the voices of men hushed, he had meditated upon God till the spiritual had become the actual. The thoughts that arose in his heart were, he felt, not his own. They came as though spoken in audible words by God. I do not suppose there was a literal voice, but it was to Moses as though it were so. Is it wonderful that Moses was carried above his ordinary self? His whole nature was elevated into a loftier world. Like Paul, he heard " unspeakable words." They filled him with reverence and awe, delight and joy. He saw the truth; he felt that God had revealed to him the everlasting law of righteousness. He was " inspired," as we say, in the deepest recesses of his spirit.

Now the miracle was in the revelation of God to Moses. The shining face followed on that as a necessary consequence. Our faces would have shone if we had been there; not, perhaps, as

Moses' did, because we are of a poorer and meaner
nature, but as much as they are capable of
shining.   Love makes the face shine; happy
thought makes the face shine; a word with old
friends makes the face shine.   No wonder that
Moses' face shone when he looked upon the Source
of all joy and blessedness and communed with
the Infinite Spirit.   A shining face, therefore, is
the appropriate expression of a happy, peaceful,
inspiring religion—a religion full of love to God
and of service to man.   To have a shining face is
to live in the presence of God, and to radiate His
blessed influence on those around us.   If this is so,
it is a most important acquirement for you and
me.   Let us look at it.

And notice what it is that a shining face expresses.   If you and I could have looked into the
face of Moses, what should we have seen there?

A quickened intelligence.   Moses was a man of
genius, as we say.   He had a wide sweep of
thought, a keen and vivid insight.   It is not easy
to say at this distance of time how much of the
books attributed to him were actually written by
him.   We know that they were edited by others
again and again, and probably altered in the
editing.   But the mere fact that he has stamped
his name on them shows that he was a man of
vast power.   Men do not attribute the best things
in their best books to fools or weaklings.   If you
want to know what Moses was, read that wonder-

ful thirty-second chapter of Deuteronomy: "My doctrine shall drop as the rain, my speech shall distil as the dew," &c. Or read the nineteenth Psalm: "Lord, Thou hast been our dwelling-place in all generations." But this fine intelligence of Moses was enlarged and quickened beyond measure when he came into actual relation with God. He put on a greatness and power not his own. He went up into the mount Moses; he came down Moses still, but filled, as some of us would like to be, "with all the fulness of God." Believe me, there is no quickener of intelligence like communion with God. I have seen a man, poor in education, dull in expression, ordinary in mind, till he has awakened to his relation with God; and that has meant the awakening of his entire consciousness. You know there is nothing that stimulates intellect like the contact with other intellects. Education means this: it means the bringing of the young mind under the influence of minds that know better and think more powerfully than they do. If you want to unfold your mind, get into contact with a nobler mind. A man of wider sympathies and purer aims enlarges our souls, as the sunlight and the rain bring out the blossoms. And surely the Infinite Mind can do as much for us. He can fill us with light; "for God is light, and in Him is no darkness at all." Men are telling us now that we cannot know God. They have invented a long word for their new theory:

they call it Agnosticism. And when a man has
talked a little about Agnosticism, and called himself an Agnostic, he feels that he is quite a philosopher.

Meanwhile, my friends, it remains true that
he who communes with his God in secret, as
Moses did, understands all things with a deeper
wisdom. "The secret of the Lord is with them
that fear Him"; and when God tells us His secret,
we find it the key to all other secrets. Not know
God? Blessed be His name, it is too late in the
day to tell some of us that! We have known Him
for ten, twenty, thirty years; and we are as sure
of Him as we are of friend and brother, of wife and
child. That He *is*, and that He is *Love*, we know;
and that knowledge puts all other knowledge in
a new and blessed light. It quickens our knowledge of nature till the world glistens in the light
of it. The stars that gem the midnight sky, the
flowers that spring in our pathway, the forest
sanctuary, and the great and wide sea, all speak
to us of the brightness and beauty of God, and
their own interest is increased thereby a thousand-
fold. It quickens our knowledge of man too.
What a dreary waste would human life and history be if there were no wisdom and no love over it
all! Take away the Fatherly eye that watches us,
that guides us, that looks lovingly down upon us,
and you take away the very meaning of life. If
you shut out God, you shut out truth and

righteousness and hope, and take the significance from existence. For what is truth but the thought of God? what is righteousness but the will of God? what is hope but our confidence that Divine love and wisdom will bring all right at last?

" God's in His heaven ; all's right with the world,"

as Robert Browning makes his little peasant-girl sing. So far from Agnosticism raising us in the scale of creation, it is the knowledge of Him that gives life and meaning to all other knowledge. Science without God is a mere rattle of dry bones ; history is a mournful drama without plot or purpose ; poetry and literature are the meaningless amusements of men doomed to speedy extinction ; the world is a jumble of atoms, aimlessly brought together : and man himself a ghastly riddle, with no key or solution. Go up into the mount of God, my brother, for light and truth and wisdom ; for if you would have the radiance of knowledge in your eyes, you must have the inspiration of God in your heart.

This is true also of the lesser facts of life. We shall understand them if we know God—and only then. If our lives are ordered for us by Him, there is still mystery, but there is no contradiction. The joys and sorrows of every day—its work, its rest, its success and failure, its annoyance and gratification, are each part of the " all things that work together for good." To the man who com-

munes with God, the will of his Heavenly Father
constitutes a sufficient theory of life. What I do
not know, God knows, and He will reveal all need-
ful truth to me, as I am able to bear it.

*A shining face reveals also an awakened conscience,
as well as a quickened intelligence.* Faces shine with
goodness as well as with knowledge. Indeed that
is the softest and sweetest radiance of all. It is,
of course, a benign and cheerful goodness that
shines. I suppose Moses when he came down
from the mount was full of joy. He had stood
face to face with the fountain of all joy and
goodness. And we, if we are awakened to Him,
ought to have our whole nature transfigured with
joy. "Rejoice in the Lord alway," says the
Apostle, and, as if he could not be too emphatic,
he repeats, "Again I say rejoice." We think of
an awakened conscience as though it were an
element of dread. But why should it be so? Is
not God's righteousness a glorious fact—the very
hope and salvation of the world? For it is a loving
righteousness, a redemptive righteousness, delight-
ing not in condemnation, but in forgiveness; a
righteousness which is embodied in Christ, and
therefore is on our side, and not against us at
all. A Christian man should be a fountain of joy
to all about him.

> "When one who holds communion with the skies
> Has filled his urn where those pure waters rise,
> Descends and dwells amongst us meaner things,
> It is as if an angel shook his wings."

Let us away with a gloomy, sour-faced type of piety. It has frozen the buds of holiness in thousands of young souls. And, on the other hand, a quiet, loving, cheerful goodness is more likely to make others good than a hundred sermons. We want a sweeter, more attractive goodness amongst us. We want less of fault-finding, and more of the love " that hopeth all things, and believeth all things." Anybody can find fault. It is the cheapest and poorest kind of criticism. It requires a far keener and truer eye to discern excellencies than it does to find defects. It would be a good thing for us all if we admired each other more ; we should love each other better, and grow in goodness and graciousness more rapidly.

Think of Christ, I pray you, who would not even " break the bruised reed, nor quench the smoking flax," but went about everywhere raising up the fallen, supporting the weak, and redeeming the lost. Imagine St. John, the apostle of love, sitting in the midst of a select coterie and amusing himself by picking out the defects in his neighbours, holding them up to ridicule and scorn, or, still worse, magnifying their sins and actual wrong-doing ! Oh, beloved, a harsh word has often ruined a soul ! The *best* men are gentle, charitable, easy to be entreated, long-suffering, kind. They carry with them a hopeful, shining face. It is not the sullen sky, racked with angry clouds, that gives life ; it is the kiss of the morning sun that awakens the birds to their song and the flowers to their beauty. And a man may well look radiant who sees the beauty of holiness. Keep near, then, to Christ. See how grand He is; let "His gentleness make you great;" and your face will shine with so sweet and inspiring a radiance that other men will feel its power and will be drawn to Him too.

A shining face means also a great love. Nothing is like love to make the face shine. "We needs must love the highest when we see it," and Moses saw the highest. His face shone with brightness because his heart glowed with love. What a power a love like that would have to elevate and inspire our lives also. Nothing short of love can do it. Love is the greatest propelling power that actuates all forms of human greatness. What carried martyrs to the stake? Love for a great cause. What makes a man die in battle, and never feel the pain? Love to his country. One of the sweetest words in history is that which tells us how Jacob served for Rachel seven years, "and they seemed to him but a few days," for the love he bore her. That story goes very deep. It shows how love can so inspire a man as to turn pain into pleasure. They say, and I believe them, that many of the martyrs felt no pain. A mighty love for Christ was what they felt, and it overpowered every other emotion. So it would be with us if we could love Him thus; duty would become inspira-

tion, and we should suffer joyfully. There is a
world of power in the Apostle's words: "For *Thy*
sake we are killed all the day long." Remember
what Tennyson says of the soldier's wife—

> "Thy voice is heard through rolling drums,
> 　That beat to battle where he stands;
> Thy face across his fancy comes,
> 　And gives the battle to his hands.

> "A moment, while the trumpets blow,
> 　He sees his brood about thy knee;
> The next, like fire he meets the foe,
> 　And strikes him dead for thine and thee."

"Many waters cannot quench love," says that
sweet love-poem, the Song of Solomon. Even of
human love this is true; and, depend upon it, the
love of man for God is a power not less mighty.
It is mighty in the man himself. It lifts him
above the sordid cares of life. His gaze is upward
instead of downward, till he becomes like Him
upon whom he looks. And it is mighty over
others. Do you desire to spread the glorious
flame? Do you wish your friends to love Him?
Would you gladly see your children growing up in
that love, breathing it as they breathe the fragrant air of the spring-time? Then let your own
face shine with it. Let it radiate from your whole
being. Make those about you feel how dear God
is to you, and He will become dear to them. A

peaceful, radiant piety is the best and purest means of doing good. Believe me, there is no way of *doing* good half so effective as *being* good; and goodness is like living seed—it grows wherever it falls, it strikes its roots in every soil, and it bears fruit, too, "thirty, sixty and a hundredfold."

But some one may ask me, "How is this higher and quickened life produced? If a shining face means a quickened life, how are we to get the quickening?"

Our text gives or implies the answer. We are to get it as Moses did, by contact with God. The passage says that it came while he talked with God. A better translation is, "*through* his talking with Him." It is the touch of the infinite and perfect Spirit that gives the lesser and finite spirit new life. Can we get such a touch? Will God look on us as He looked on Moses? Assuredly He will. He is not only life in Himself, but the fountain of life to others. It is His delight to give, and to give this very thing—His own energy and power. Our sorrow and our defect is our lifelessness. We have just life enough to feel that we are dead, as compared with what we might be. And yet that very sense of impotence, if we use it rightly, is our truest blessing. It is the voice of God in our souls, crying to us to come to Him that He may give us life. Oh, dull, weary faces, in which there is no light, go up into the mount of communion, I pray you, and you shall return transfigured and shining, with a lustre not your own, but radiant with the light and inspiration of God !

THEOLOGICAL.

I

THE CREED OF THE AGNOSTIC.

"Ye worship ye know not what." (*Authorized Version.*)
"Ye worship that which ye know not." (*Revised Version.*)
—JOHN iv. 22.

THESE are words of Christ to the woman of Samaria. They sound a little harsh as we first listen to them. But, as always with Christ, the harshness is only on the surface—there is an infinite depth of pity and tenderness beneath. Christ wants to draw this woman away from a poor, narrow idea of God to a larger and more living conception. He wants to draw her from the notion of one who had done nothing for men to the belief in Him who had revealed Himself as a Saviour. "The salvation"—not, observe, salvation in general, as though only Jews could be saved, but *the* salvation, the salvation of all men everywhere—is of or from the Jews. It is promised to them, and springs from them. They therefore worship a God whom they know—whom they know as forgiveness, love, deliverance; whom they know as the Father and Friend of them and of all men. Not so the Samaritans. To them God was a somewhat indifferent and distant Being, holding no living relation towards them. He was a mere product of abstract thought, without any true significance. Christ intimates this by the word He uses: "Ye worship ye know not *what*," or "*that* which ye know not." "What" is neuter, and "that" has the same implication, designating something without what we call personality—without a mind to think, or a will to guide, or a heart to love—a formless, indefinite, shadowy uncertainty, which can satisfy no man's intellect, and in which no man can find rest for his soul. Christ calls her away from that to the true and eternal God.

Now it is in just a similar position that we find those who to-day are called Agnostics. Agnostic means one who does not know. It is from *A*, not, and *gnôsticos*, one who is capable of knowing. The creed of the Agnostic may be stated in a few words. He says that God cannot be known. He dare not deny that there is a First Being, one from whom all others spring. He says it may be so— nay, it seems to him it must be so. But he declares we do not and cannot know anything about such a Being except the bare fact that He, or rather it, exists. We have no faculties by which we can understand any attributes or qualities which He may possess. Is He, or it, infinite? We cannot grasp infinity. Is it eternal? We are overwhelmed and confounded by the bare notion of eternity. Is it morally good? There is no meaning in saying so of any but a limited and finite being like ourselves, one who can come into definite relations with other beings also finite and limited. In short, we know nothing of the First Being, except that there is one, and that He is the underlying cause and reality of the universe. I believe that to be a just description of the Agnostic's creed. He is not an atheist. He does not say there is no God. He feels that such an assertion is a perilous and tremendous negative. As Foster said, it would require a man to travel all over the universe and examine everything in it to be sure it did not contain the evidence of a God. But a man may say, " I do not know," and it may appear only a modest, and almost a reverent, attitude, a patient waiting for evidence, appropriate to the condition of a mortal, and corresponding to the narrowness of his powers.

Let me say also that as the Agnostic does not believe in God, he has no hope for the future. Death is to him the final end of man.

Now, I am not about to enter on a philosophical argument with the Agnostic. That can be done, and, as I believe, done conclusively. The philosophy of Agnosticism is not a profound philosophy. The great minds of all the ages are against it. Plato knew it and rejected it. Socrates thought it worthy only of children and savages. Aristotle confuted

it in detail. And in modern times the great men
have been against it too. Locke and Berkeley,
Reid and Stewart, Descartes and Malebranche,
Kant and Fichte, Schelling and Hegel have all flung
it away. It owes its present popularity mainly to
one name—that of Mr. Herbert Spencer. I do not
deny—of course I do not—that Mr. Spencer is an
able, and even a great man. But many a great
man has held a poor and shallow philosophy. I
say it respectfully, but I say it firmly, that it is
not as a philosopher that Mr. Spencer appears to
me to be great. He has a brilliant scientific
imagination, and a most impressive literary style.
He is, moreover, a master of cogent statement, and
of the forms of logical debate; but as a philosopher he is not in the first rank. He is only
just now the fashion, which is quite a different
thing. Twenty years ago Carlyle was the fashion;
now he is almost underrated. Ten years ago Mr.
Mill was the fashion; now his reputation, like an
old coat, is a little out at elbows. And the day
will come when Mr. Spencer will be more calmly
judged; perhaps—such is the oddity of human
caprice—when he will be rated at less than his real
worth. Of course I do not desire that. I only
desire that those who listen to me now should not
be dazzled by the glamour of a celebrated name.
Give it its due, but keep the balance of your own
judgment. Be of the mind of the old Greek
thinker who said, when some one was trying to

quote him down with Plato, " Plato is my friend, but truth is more so still."

People will come to see some day that if I can know that something exists, and that it is a cause, I may also know much more about it. Existence and causation are human ideas, and if they apply to it there is no conceivable reason why other ideas should not apply to it also. If I know that anything exists, and is a cause, I may also know it as good, and vile, and mighty, if it really be so. It is a question of evidence—that, and only that. And the evidence for a good and holy God is large and rich. I admit that it is not such as to *force* belief. A man may, if he will, reject it. But meanwhile it is abundant. It is in the outward world. " The heavens declare the glory of God, and the firmament showeth His handiwork." It is here, too, in our own conscience. Our conscience is the voice of God; it speaks, not in its own name, but in the name of eternal righteousness and truth. It is in all history too. History is the long record of the righteous rulership of God in the world. It is the living proof that there is a Judge and a Ruler who is determined to overthrow falsehood and folly, tyranny and vice, and to give the victory to justice and truth, integrity and purity. The motto which might be written on the scroll of history is the terrible sentence of Scripture, " Be sure your sin will find you out." It is one long witness to the steady rulership of God—a rulership gentle and tender indeed, but strong and firm, "forgiving iniquity, transgression, and sin, but by no means clearing the guilty."

But I am not attempting to *argue* with the Agnostic. I am willing enough to do so, given the proper time and place. At present, however, I want to look at his position as a *creed*. A creed is a belief by which a man proposes to live and die. It offers itself as a basis of true thinking, right acting, and healthy feeling. It says, "Believe as I teach you, do as I tell you, guide your feelings into the directions I point out to you, and your life shall be noble and good—at the very least it shall be as pure and satisfactory as, in an imperfect state like this, human life can be made." Now it is as a creed that I criticize the Agnostic's belief. He gives me nothing to *live* by, nothing to *work for*, nothing to *die by*. He takes all the dignity and worth out of life, and leaves it a poor, senseless enigma. See how this is true.

I. The Agnostic creed gives us no *moral basis* for our life. Of course I do not mean that every Agnostic is an immoral man. So far is that from being true, that some of them are among the noblest men I know. But they are so by something like an inconsistency. For there is no *ultimate* reason, no basis in the Agnostic creed on which a noble moral life reposes. If there is a God who is good and righteous, if my conscience is a ray of light derived from Him, if the universe is built by a righteous God on unchangeable principles of justice and truth, then there is a clear and sufficient *reason* for my doing all I can to become a righteous man. I am, in fact, a "fool" if I do not. For I am fighting against all the laws of creation, against the deepest and most permanent forces of the world, if I oppose myself to righteousness. I am on one side—the whole sweep and tendency of things is on the other. I am violating my own nature and the nature of everything else. I am simply an element of disorder and chaos, opposing my feeble, foolish will to the harmony and beauty of God's glorious world. But if the power that made the world is—I know not what—if it is not good, or just, or righteous, but only a blind, deaf, unthinking, unfeeling force, with no more mind than a puff of steam, and no more conscience than a winter storm, why should I be a good man? Where is the basis for goodness? Oh, you say, think of the good of others—you should be good for their sakes! Well, yes; but again, *why?* If the good of others is committed to my care by the law of my nature, you speak reasonably; but then the power that laid that law upon me *must* be a power that *knew* what it was doing, if it has any claim to moral obedience. Think of it, I pray you, think it out to the bottom. It is not, I say, a possible thing that conscience should be a mere prejudice, that goodness should be a whim and a crotchet; and yet, if that be not true, the law that

conscience reveals *must* be the law, not of an
unthinking force, but of an intelligent and righteous God.   It is of no use to tell me that society
is the lawgiver.   Society!   Who gave society a
right over you and me?   If it has a right, and no
doubt it has, that right must repose on some law
of nature; it must spring from the Power that made
not only me, but society also.   Society is no ultimate source of authority.   What has society that
it did not receive?   Push your question back, and
back, and back, and you come to this—either there
is no basis for the moral life at all, or that basis is
laid, firm and strong, in the eternal and unalterable
character of the great First Cause, the just and
righteous God.   Now I say that it is a fatal objec-
tion to Agnosticism *as a creed.*   Young men, I speak
to you.   Your first business is to *live*, not to argue, or
to speculate; to *be*, not to talk.   And, if you are to
live, you must have some view of the world and of
life which will form a foundation on which you may
build, a starting-point from which you may set out.
The gospel gives you one.   It gives you the
infinite and holy God for your Father, the sacred
and perfect Christ for your Saviour and your
Friend.   You will not find life an easy process.
You will be racked with anxiety, torn by conflicting
passions, and sometimes so fiercely tempted that your
integrity and your whole moral life will be toppling
on the verge of the precipice of ruin.   I offer you
a creed to live by.   It will make you strong if you

really believe it. It has carried thousands over to victory, and those the best and noblest souls in all the past. Agnosticism is no such creed. The bottom is out of it, before it begins. Take the better and the nobler. You are surely safe in doing so. For that which is good and pure and noble *must be* also true.

II. Again, Agnosticism gives no account of the meaning and rational purpose of human life. Why are you and I here? What is the purpose for which we were born? What is the design of our advent into the world? What is the end which we are to pursue, which it is wise and good to seek? If we can answer these questions we shall in part, at least, unriddle the mystery of the life within and around us. We shall know why we suffer so much, why we are tempted by evil, why we fall, why we are permitted to taste the bitter conse- quences of our own folly and self-will. The gospel does reply to these inquiries of our souls. It tells us, to quote venerable words, that the reason and purpose of our being here is that we may " glorify God and enjoy Him for ever." It cries as Augustine does, " O God, Thou hast made us for Thyself, and our hearts are restless till they find rest in Thee." It tells us that all our suffering and pain, all our weakness and want, nay, our very sin itself, is permitted that we may learn the evil of evil, and the good of good, and so grow up into Christ, and God, and holiness. That idea of a special purpose

under and around our life, a Divine leading and
teaching, ever watchful, ever loving, ever bringing
light out of darkness and good out of evil, is the
profound and satisfactory solution of the sorrow
and the mystery through which we pass.   What
matter suffering if there is an end and a purpose—
a glorious end and a Divine purpose in what we
suffer ?   What matter mystery if the mystery is
about to burst and disclose the splendour of perfect
knowledge and completed goodness ?   I am a child
at school.   The lesson may be hard and the flogging
severe—but the result is worth it all.   But what
does Agnosticism say to all this ?   It tells me that
these questions which my spirit asks can have no
answer.   Why am I here ? why do I suffer ? why
is my progress so slow, and wisdom so long in
coming ? There *is no why*, says Agnosticism. Human
life has no purpose, no meaning, no result.   It is a
wave on the sea, a bubble on the fountain, a mist
in the air, here to-day and gone to-morrow, leaving
no result behind.   You suffer because you cannot
help it—no good result comes out of it.   You strive,
and fail, and there is no eye to pity and no arm to
save.   That is the gospel of Agnosticism !   Is it a
creed for a *man*, I ask you, or is it not rather a
creed for a heartless savage, or an unthinking
animal ?   Can you and I—creatures with memory
and hope—live by that ?   Or is it not rather a
combination of heart-breaking tragedy and be-
wildering confusion ?   What value is there in a

creed which leaves unanswered all the deepest and loftiest questions of life—all the questions indeed which we really care to ask.

> " Oh ! somewhere, somewhere God unknown,
>   Exist and be;
>   I am dying; I am all alone ;
>   I must have Thee ! "

will still be the cry of the human soul in the midst of the mystery of life.

III. Agnosticism, too, leaves us without hope for the future of the human race. It is strange that this should be so, for no word will be found so frequently on the lips of an Agnostic as the word progress. He is always talking of the progress of the world, and pointing to the glories of a future when all religion, or, as he calls it, superstition, shall be overthrown, and science shall have converted the earth into a paradise of comfort and convenience. But on what is his hope founded ? Oh, he answers, on the analogy of the past. Man *has* made progress, and I therefore believe he will do so still. But wait a moment, my friend. If there is no reason, no love, no providence in the government of the universe, if it is all blind and without intelligence, *why* should things continue to grow better ? Why should they not cease by some sudden catastrophe ? Why, for example, should not the earth meet suddenly some dark planet wandering through space and dash to pieces against

14

it? Or, again, why should not the progress of
man culminate now, or next year, and then begin
to decline, till misery and barbarism return and
become universal? To do them justice, some of
our Agnostics feel the force of this reasoning, and
think it likely that something of the kind will
actually take place. Dr. Maudsley, for instance,
thinks the earth will grow cold at the centre, till it
becomes all but uninhabitable, and only a few
half-frozen, shivering men, without hair and without
teeth, will huddle together in the region near the
equator. At last even they will perish, and the
earth will swing, a lifeless, icy mass, round the
deserted sun. This is the gospel of Agnosticism as
to the future of the world. Not much there to kindle
enthusiasm! No strong stimulus in that to
sustain our faith and hope as we work for the
future of our oppressed and sorrowing world! No,
sirs, I tell you *that* is no creed to make men brave
and strong.

Now, open the Bible. What is this that falls on
our ears, this sweet music of prophetic song, old,
yet ever new? Listen: "And it shall come to
pass, in the last days, that the mountain of the
Lord's house shall be established in the top of the
mountains, and shall be exalted above the hills, and
all nations shall flow unto it. . . . And (the Lord)
shall judge among the nations, and shall rebuke
many people, and they shall beat their swords into
ploughshares and their spears into pruning-hooks,

nation shall not lift up sword against nation, neither shall they learn war any more." Do you tell me that even the Bible speaks of an end to the earth and a final close of human history? I know it does. But the Bible also speaks of meaning and purpose in it all. It speaks of a day when God shall gather out of His kingdom all that worketh abomination and maketh a lie, when He shall give the kingdom to His righteous Son. Still more. The view of the Bible is not bounded, as that of the Agnostic is, by this present world. It looks beyond the grave. Though the earth pass away, though the heavens disappear, though the material universe be no more, there is, if the Bible be true, "A new heaven and a new earth wherein dwelleth righteousness." Our view, therefore, is not closed in by earth and time, it expands into eternity. There is a future for man. There is a future for you—for us all.

Thus you have before you the two creeds—the creed of the Agnostic, the hope of the Christian. Which will you choose? Will you live a "know-nothing" in all that it really concerns man to know? Or will you grasp the nobler faith and trust the larger hope? Will you turn in earnest to Christ, and walk by the light of His gospel, and so lay up for yourself a boundless treasure in Him? That, as I cannot but think, is the wiser part; yes, and the truer part as well. He who believes in Christ with all his heart, so as to live in consistency with his belief, has built his house upon the rock. I know there are clouds of doubt around our generation. I know there are storms of unbelief beating on many an honest and honourable mind. Yet I am not doubtful of the result. " The rain descended, and the winds blew, and beat upon that house ; and it fell not, for it was founded upon a rock."

II

THEOLOGY AND RELIGION.

" Canst thou by searching find out God ? "—Job xi. 7.
" I had heard of Thee by the hearing of the ear, but now mine eye seeth Thee."—Job xlii. 5.

THESE two verses tell us very much of the relation between Theology and Religion. The first, though taken from a speech of Zophar, who was on the whole mistaken, yet hints at a truth both obvious and profound. The second is the cry of the delivered spirit who sees God face to face and lives. The first expresses real yet imperfect knowledge of Theology ; the second, the triumphant experience of Religion. Both know, but they know in different ways. Both are good, but the second only is essential.

Theology is the knowledge of God. It is a word constructed like many other words with which we are now familiar. It ends in the syllable "ology," which is the common designation of a science. Ge-ology is the science of the earth ; Bi-ology is

the science of living creatures; Physi-ology is the
science of the processes which go on in the bodies
of plants and animals.   Theology is the science or
knowledge of God.

But a certain school of modern thought asserts
that Theology is impossible.   It says that we can
have no knowledge of God at all; certainly none
of a scientific character.   It tells us, in the distasteful words of Comte, that the "heavens declare
no other glory than the glory of Kepler and
Newton," and that the telescope sweeps the
heavens, and the microscope penetrates the intimate structure of natural objects, and neither of
them finds a God.   Science, we are told, allows
us to conceive of many other ways in which the
universe may have originated besides those of
intelligence and design.   In fact, a group of
thinkers and writers, by no means small, says
No to us when we say that we find God in all
things, and are able to trace the indications of His
skill and of the methods by which He works.

And yet even this school of teachers does not
propose to abolish religion.   Theology is to go;
but religion is to remain.   Nay, more; there are
some who say that when we have no Theology our
religion will be better and more elevating than
ever.   If we did not live in a time when it is
no longer possible to surprise us, we should be
astonished at such a proposition.   But there are
actually men who think that a world—or rather the

unknown force that created it—without thought, without love, without will, without any noble quality of which we can form even a bare conception, forms a more appropriate object of reverence and devotion than our Father which is in heaven. They propose to retain religion after they have dethroned God. As well try to breathe in a vacuum, or to fly without wings. So common sense seems to say; so experience also in part declares. And yet, while we reject their theory, let us think charitably of the writers. They have denied God in words, but they have honoured Him in fact. They have been better than their meagre creed. They have unconsciously invested the blind force they worshipped with the love and pity of God; or have taken up the human race to which they were devoted into an ideal humanity like that of Christ. In other words, being good and noble men, they could not put away the Deity whom their hearts loved, even when their philosophy bade them, any more than men can sweep away the sea or extinguish the light of the sun.

This strange position, however, starts the question, What is the relation of Theology to Religion? Are they the same? Or, if different, are they of equal importance? How are we to use them for the elevation of our character and the guidance of our life? Of course I cannot exhaust so vast a subject now. I can only indicate some starting-points of thought—seeds that may grow if you water them by quiet thought, and warm the air around them by trustful prayer. Do so, my younger friends. I *alone* cannot help you; I can only help you to help yourselves. Notice, then—

I. Theology is necessary to religion as an embodiment is to life. Theology we have defined as the knowledge of God. Religion we may also define, though it is never easy to put the greatest powers and influences of our being into a form of words. It will, however, be enough for our purpose now if we say that religion is made up of reverence, admiration, and love. To worship is to admire and to love, and to have the reverence that makes us willing to obey. Now it is clear that we can only admire and love on the basis of some degree of knowledge. Let me know *nothing* of one of the heroes of history, and I shall be quite indifferent to him. It may be true that religion is mainly emotion, so that love, passionate admiration, and the perfect obedience that cries, " Father, not my will but Thine be done," are the soul of it ; it is still true that these feelings must be set in some framework of knowledge, or there is nothing to call them forth. In fact, we cannot divide the functions and activities of our nature absolutely. There is knowledge in all emotion, and emotion in almost all knowledge. They have a vital connection, like the body and the soul. Knowledge produces feeling, and thus feeling increases knowledge. It is love that opens the eyes to see good qualities, but it is the presence of the good qualities that kindles and increases love.

Notice, however, that in the religious life knowledge holds the subordinate place. Theology is of value only as the cause or condition of religion. The essential thing is the life of our will and affections; and the kind of knowledge we need is such only as elevates and intensifies these. Theology can never be any more than a means to religion as an end. Take careful notice of what I am saying, for it is just here that some of the greatest mistakes have been made. Theology has been cultivated for its own sake. It has been used as in itself an interesting occupation of the human intellect. It has ceased to be a servant, and stolen the robe and crown of a queen. And so it has forgotten its place. Two consequences have followed —it has grown tyrannical, and it has grown helpless. Tyrannical—for it has restrained the thoughts of men and lowered their lives. Think of Bunyan's giant Pope sitting in his cave and mumbling at the pilgrims whom he can no longer burn or imprison. Think of good men and godly women pining in gaols, or burned in the midst of the public market. The old Roman poet Lucretius saw the tyrannical tendency of Theology when she forgets her proper place, and turned from her with disgust. Helpless, too, is an encroaching Theology, for she raises questions that no man can answer. She asks concerning God what she can never know.

What is the *essence* of God? Tell me the essence of a star or a stone and I will answer you. What is the manner of God's existence? I do not know, nor do you; and the profoundest philosopher is as ignorant as we. The one thing, the only one, which we can know of God, and at the same time the only one that we need to know, is His *character*. He unites perfect love with infinite power and absolute wisdom. Know that, and see His love and wisdom in the face of Jesus Christ. Trace them in your own lives. Feel them speaking in your hearts. The knowledge of God we need is such a knowledge as is given in experience. That knowledge is of His character, His mighty love that conquers our sin and extirpates all evil.

It lights up history in the story of the Cross. It gives us the assurance that we are not alone in a world where sin and sorrow are so intertwined with life that we look in vain for an explanation and a hope. Rest *there*, my brother. The hope is in Christ, in the fact that He reveals and interprets the heart of God. And the explanation will come when all things yield up their secret in the clear light of the final day.

II. Theology is less than religion. Our knowledge is less than our love and trust. Knowledge is always less than its objects. All science is so. Astronomy does not know *all* about the sun and the stars, and, it is safe to say, never will. Physi-ology knows not more than a fragment of the mysterious gathering and balance of forces that make up the life of the body. There is not the smallest thing in nature that is exhaustively known. It is not wonderful, therefore, that God is more than we know of Him. And because we are conscious that our knowledge can never measure God in any of His great qualities, therefore our love and trust outrun our knowledge ; our religion outruns our theology. Even in human relations this is true. Husband and wife ensphere each other in a halo of love and trust without waiting for complete knowledge. Oh, you are a poor, pitiful soul if your love does not "trust where it cannot trace "! For, see, if you do not trust on a little knowledge you will never get any more. I can never show my true self to any one who does not already love me, nor can you. It is when God and His Christ are taken on credit, as it were, that they unfold the deepest aspects of their character. Love with a little knowledge, and you will soon arrive at more. Here is the reason why a true theology must always be a progressive one. Even in regard to the character and attributes of God the eye, cleared by love, will be always receiving new revelation. And this is true of the eye of the Church as well as of the individual. We *do* make progress in theology. We have made progress since men drew up the unintelligible contradictions of the Athanasian Creed. We have made progress since good souls wasted their time in defining the inward constitution of the Trinity. We have made progress since we ceased to believe that infants were flagrant sinners, and drew a distinction between inherited defect and the wrath of God. No, you cannot go back. There are doctrines that once dead, are dead for ever. They were pushed off the tree of faith by a life new and large—the life that made us see that the goodness of man is only a faint shadow of that of God, so that the heavens shall fall rather than He do a cruelty or a wrong. The science or knowledge of God grows out of the knowledge of His works, whether in nature or in man. As history grows, as science, in the narrower sense, grows, as government becomes more just and pure, as the Bible is more minutely studied, and better compared with other sacred books, so shall we have a greater idea of God, and therefore practically worship a nobler Deity.

III. Theology would otherwise be destructive of religion. It often has been. When our knowledge of God—our supposed knowledge—has stiffened and shrivelled, our religion has had no room to grow, and then one of two things has happened: either our religion has broken our theology, and moulded it again on a larger pattern; or religion has been strangled, and for the time killed. The great danger of maintaining old dogmas which have lost their living power lies just here: If you maintain them you are likely to send thinking men away into misery and unbelief. Those who cry out about our deserting the doctrines of Calvin, may think they are defending Christ and pleading for His truth. But they are not; they are doing something as far from that as the poles are from the equator. They are compelling men—many of whom have a great hungering for God, and would gladly believe—to give up their faith in Christ, and sink into the dreary gulf of Atheism. The doctrines of Calvin about the Divine decrees suited his hard, cold, blood-stained time. Men could stand calmly by and see the flesh of Servetus fall roasted to cinders with the roaring flame. No wonder that the same men could believe in the damnation of infants, and in the eternal loss of all but a few specially selected from our doomed and hated race. But we cannot do that now. We cannot rejoice that we are saved at the expense or to the neglect of other men. We can rather doubt the existence of God than charge Him with actions which we should resent as an insult if alleged against ourselves. We feel the force of the words of Bacon : " I would rather men should say there was no Bacon than 1 would that they should declare that there was one Bacon who devoured his own children." We feel that if the gospel is a good news such as we can receive it must reveal a God and a Saviour whom we can recognize as good and just. " The decree," said Calvin himself, " is horrible but true." " No," we reply, " if the decree is horrible it cannot be true." If it comes from the Eternal Goodness it must not aggravate our perplexity and shock our conscience; it must tend, at least, to scatter the clouds of our darkness and reveal the dayspring from on high. Thank God, it does. Christ is light—" the light that lighteth every man." Christ is love—the perfect love of God manifest in the flesh. Christ is salvation, first from the power and the love of sin, and then from the consequences of sin now and for ever.

IV. Another word. Theology must be scientific. I cannot tell you all I mean by that now. But in the main I mean that it must be built upon facts which men can see for themselves and can verify— find true—in actual experience. Theology must be open, without fear and without favour, to all new light, from whatever source it may come. It must not waste its time in confuting Darwin, or arguing against the last scientific theory; it must do its own work. It must show man to himself as needing God and able to find rest in Him alone. It must take away the wrappings from the face of Christ and let us see Him as He was on earth and always is—the heart of God poured forth for the deliverance of man. It must bring to light all the truth *about* Scripture, and *in* Scripture, with a firm and fearless utterance. It must believe, and act on the belief, that nothing but good can come from truth—a proposition that must be true if God is behind the facts of the universe—so that to doubt it is Atheistic. If all this is done we shall have a scientific theology.

Meanwhile, you and I must not wait for a complete theology, for theology will never be complete. Life is passing. Time is slipping away. We want a spiritual home while we live and work here. We want a future which will give point and meaning to our work, and crown it with immortality. Science? Oh, yes, by all means; but if science blot out the face of God and take away the hope of a future and a better life, "What matters science unto men?" You must have more than science to live the life of a man, looking into the past and future, with "thoughts that wander through eternity." Look, then, at Christ. Let Him pour His life into your spirit. I ask you to believe no terrible dogmas. I would not for a moment set aside the authority of your own reason and judgment, or induce you to violate your conscience. Only, I beseech you, study Christ, and be at the same time true to your best self; and I think you will not find it possible to turn away from Him. Theology can tell us much about God, but it is, after all, cold and abstract, and often imperfect and stammering, like a report at second-hand. But he who knows and loves Christ can say, "I have heard of Thee by the hearing of the ear, but now mine eye seeth Thee."

III.

" Christ, the power of God, and the wisdom of God.'
—1 Cor. i. 24.

THIS is what St. Paul preached both to Jews and Greeks. It was not at first sight after their taste. The Greeks sought rather a philosophy —a complete theory of life. They liked to see the universe of man and nature spread out before them —a consistent, rational, magnificent whole. The Jews sought for signs. They were looking for their Messiah – their Deliverer and King—and they wanted his credentials. Paul brought neither philosophy nor credentials. He proclaimed a poor, outcast, and crucified Messiah. To the Greek this was folly. To the Jew it was incredible, as being the exact opposite of what he expected. And yet among both Jews and Greeks there were a few— men of deeper insight and larger heart—who saw then more than philosophy and more than a thousand credentials : " Christ, the power of God, and the wisdom of God."

And so it is still. We have now a far wider circle of comparison than St. Paul. He knew no religious teachers but those of Greece, or Rome, or Judea. We know the religions of many nations, both ancient and still existing. Our best scholars teach us what were the religions of Assyria, of Babylon, of Persia, of Egypt, of India, of China. And we find after examining all these that we can still say, " Christ crucified is greater." He is, in a sense that they are not, " the power of God, and the wisdom of God." Not that we wish to under-rate them. Not that they are, as we used to say, " false " religions. We admit gladly that they contain great truths. They shed much light, true light, on the world, on life, and on death. We doubt not that many have walked in that light so as to live nobly and die peacefully. And we remember that " in *every* nation he that feareth God and doeth righteousness is accepted with Him." Still those different religions are not all that man needs. They are not " the power of God, and the wisdom of God."

Of course I cannot examine them all this morning. The study of " Comparative Religion," as we now call it, is as vast as it is interesting. The young men and women amongst us who are thirsty for knowledge can take it up with great profit. The great master of it in England is Professor Max Müller of Oxford; our own Dr. Fairbairn also is deeply learned in the same line of study. But

15

we can only take what I may call specimen religions
now.   There are three that I choose because, first,
they are specially important ; and, secondly, they
are professed by millions of our own fellow-sub-
jects in India and elsewhere : they are Hinduism,
Buddhism, and Mohammedanism.   These are
amongst the chief religions of the world, outside
our own.   They are favourable specimens; I *mean*
them to be so, so that in the light of them we
can compare Christ with other teachers.

Again, these forms of religion resemble what we
see and hear around us now.   So that the comparison between them and the teachings of Christ
is really a comparison that has relation with the
life of to-day.   You will see this as I go on.

Notice that the founders of these religions
teach only ; Jesus teaches and *embodies* His
teaching.   Buddha was a teacher, and a noble one
too.   His story is in many ways beautiful and
pathetic.   He tried to start a new and higher life
among the degenerate Hindus of his time.   Like
all reformers he suffered many things, and left the
pathos of his sufferings and the marks of the nobility
of his character on the religion which he taught.
So to a certain extent did Mohammed.   Mohammed,
however, has, I think, been too highly valued, owing
in part to the great influence of Thomas Carlyle,
who wrote of him so charmingly.   The founder of
the Vedic religion is practically unknown to us.
He lived before anything worth calling history ex-

isted, so that of him as a person we cannot speak. But neither Buddha nor Mohammed is the ideal embodiment of his own teachings. Buddha is indeed ever seeking higher righteousness and purer truth. But he *is* seeking; he has not attained. Mohammed is not even seeking. He has no doubt and no religious insight. He says now and again beautiful things of the love of virtue and the worth of duty. But the Divine charm that hangs over the person and the character of Christ is not there. Christ impresses us as above the struggle with sin; lifted into the peace which is eternal; living daily and without effort the life of truth and goodness. He is so one with His teaching that He needs no words to teach. His teaching is so one with Him that the only comment it requires is His holy and beautiful life. If Christ aspires to higher things it is with an aspiration that is fulfilled as fast as it is formed. His heart lies open to the full pulses of God's inspiration. Buddha is not at rest. Mohammed is looking for—what? Not spiritual peace; not ripened excellence; not a spirit at one with God. He is a ruler, and his one desire is for a law which will enable him to rule with effect. So that he has a sensual heaven for the obedient, and a hell of terrible torture for the disobedient. But Christ is perfectly at peace. He has no sorrow but the sorrows of others, which He bears from perfect love. The heaven He offers us is to be like Him-

self, and therefore like God. His hell is to be full of
sin and to bear the consequences which necessarily
flow from that. Christ is a ruler too, if you will,
but His rule is over the hearts and consciences of
His subjects. He founds His empire on Himself;
that is, on perfect goodness and love, and the influences flowing from them. Look, then, at this
picture as I draw it; make your choice. For although Hinduism does not appeal to you, yet
Mohammed and Buddha both do, though under
other names. There is still a religion which is
chiefly the threat of a fiery hell and the promise of
a material heaven. It gets mixed with the spiritual faith of Jesus and degrades it. There are men
yet to be found who say that the preaching of the
love of Christ produces in them a "lackadaisical
religious ease" which allows them, without dis-
comfort, to do ungodly things and to indulge in
impure practices. That is, they confess that they
are so lost to all sense of gratitude and honour towards God, as well as towards man, that they can
only be kept in decent order by the incessant
flourishing of the retributive rod. Is it so? Do
you thus do despite to the spirit of God's grace,
and count the blood of the covenant wherewith you
are sanctified an unholy thing? Is the great love
that died for you nothing? Are the agony and
bloody sweat of Gethsemane to be trampled under-
foot? Will you "crucify the Son of God afresh,
and put Him to an open shame?"—and all this be-

cause He has no pleasure in the death of a sinner, and inflicts no arbitrary punishment? Not that I would deny the fact of punishment. There is terrible punishment, only that it does not consist in an arbitrary infliction, but springs, by an eternal law, from the nature of sin itself. Hopeless shame and self-reproach, the scorn of your own conscience, the deepening sense of guilt, and so of separation from God and all good spirits; the unspeakable remorse and misery of your own mind; the hell of the sense of love refused—the protest of the soul against itself—these are your punishments here and hereafter.

Buddhism is with us to-day also. I am not speaking to the East or to the past. There are schemes of moral teaching amongst us that give you lofty and beautiful precept. But they are destitute of the first pulse of life. They do not cast out sin. They deal, as Buddhism does, in aphorisms, in wise sayings that have no power to enforce themselves. Huxley and Tyndall, Matthew Arnold and John Morley mingle their scientific and literary criticism with an abundance of admirable advice, excellent in itself and in its setting. They are masters in "the art of putting things." But Buddha is their equal on their own ground. I could easily show you that had I time to quote. Yet where is the power that draws all things to itself? Where is He who only needs to be lifted up and all men turn to Him? Do you not see that

what our souls need is not good teaching only—
nay, not even chiefly—but the power of a soul over
souls ? It is the voice that can say, "I will dwell
in you, and walk in you." Teaching alone is not
sufficient for the needs of men. For law is difficult
to be carried out. It has tremendous forces against
it. There is first what St. Paul calls "the flesh "—
our lower animal nature, a crushing power. That
starts first in our lives also, so that in addition to its
natural force it gathers the power of habit. Then
there is a fulfilment of law which is no fulfilment;
an obedience, as St. Paul says, "in the letter and
not in the spirit." You may *do* what you are told,
and yet not obey the law at all. For the law is for
the spirit, the mind and heart, as well as the
hands. Jesus was the first teacher of wisdom who
saw the remedy for that. Men had been teaching
law before they had awakened love. He reversed
the process ; He put love first and law afterwards ;
and that love might be awakened He showed the
face of God, the essence and fountain of love. He
revealed "our Father" in all the beauty of His
fatherly tenderness that we might know Him
and delight to do His will. The obedience that
flows from love is the only spiritual obedience : "If
ye *love* me keep my commandments." Do not obey
that ye may love, but love that ye may obey. This
is the meaning of the demand for love to Himself
which Jesus so constantly makes. This intensity
of love is what He means also by "eating the flesh

and drinking the blood of the Son of Man." St. Paul understood the demand and met it. He says, " I live, yet not I, but Christ liveth in me." The essential nature of Jesus must pass into and become the essential nature of His followers.

Then, when our love for God as our Father and Jesus as our Lord is fully realized, the law of love flows over to all mankind. Say what you will, man as man has had no such Saviour, no such lover as Christ. "A new commandment I give unto you," says He, " that ye love one another." " By this shall all men know that ye are my disciples." This is no narrow, paltry love for a few only. It rests on man as man. And to-day it does so in fact. The love of Christ for man is the inspiration of our deepest and noblest philanthropy. While I speak to you it is hasting with busy feet into a thousand hovels, bearing sustenance and blessing to bleeding, broken hearts. Foolish men cry out against Christianity, but take it away, and what it stands for, and a bitter wail of distress would go up to heaven from a million voices. Who freed the slave? Who gave good government to India? Who reformed the prison system? Who is moving in the hearts of noble men and women to right the wrongs of every class in the community to-day? Who sends the Salvation lassie into the lowest slums, seeking that which is lost until she find it? I say, Jesus Christ—the power of God, and the wisdom of God.

Other teachers, again, have no future to disclose
worthy of our nature and aspirations. Jesus has.
The Vedas speak of the life after death; so does
Buddha; so does Mohammed. But the future life
of the Vedas is a constant passage of the soul
from one animal into another. That of Buddha
is the same; until the highest perfection is
reached, and then the soul is supposed to sink into
" Nirvana," as it is called. It has been questioned
whether Nirvana means absolute nothingness, or
a peace and rest so profound as to be disturbed
by no thought or wish. Professor Max Müller, who
is our highest authority, settles it for us by speaking of the Buddhism of the present time as follows:
" No person who reads with attention . . . can
arrive at any other conviction than that . . . the
highest aim, the *summum bonum*, of Buddhism is
the absolute nothing." Mohammed offers his
followers a sensual heaven, where the good live
amidst fragrant odours, beautiful women, sweet
music, and the most delicate delights of all the
appetites. This, mark, is the very best that other
teachers can do. Not many weeks ago a man of
much ability, who, however, has cast off Jesus as
his guide, told me that he inclined to believe in the
transmigration of souls—*i.e.*, in their passage from
one animal body into another. And our Agnostics
are teaching us that as there is no God but one
that is unknowable, so there is no soul but one
that falls into the universal life, the Nirvana of
unconsciousness, when the body dies.

And now I ask you whether your whole soul does not turn from theories such as these to listen with a new eagerness to the voice of Christ ? " Father, I will that those whom Thou hast given me be with me where I am." " I in them, and Thou in me, that we all may be made perfect in one." " And if I go away and prepare a place for you, I will come again and receive you unto myself, that where I am there ye may be also." Yes, blessed Teacher ! it is worth while to live, it is worth while to suffer, it is worth while to die, if this is the consumma- tion Thou hast in store for us. From all other teachers, whether of the ancient or modern world, " we turn unfilled to Thee again." For Thou art not the sage of a school, nor the dreamer of a cloister ; Thou art Christ, " the wisdom of God, and the power of God" to our eager, questioning spirits.

IV.

"Go ye, therefore, and teach all nations, baptizing them in the name of the Father, and of the Son, and of the Holy Ghost."—MATT. xxviii. 19.

THAT, you see, is the revealed name. It is threefold, and yet it is one. It is variety in unity, yet unity in variety also. God has three aspects—relations, activities, powers, or what other word you will, if it be more expressive to you. Yet God is one, absolutely and completely one. There is only one ultimate ego, self, or me, in God; and Father, Word, and Holy Ghost, as distinguished from each other, are only personal, because this one absolute personality lies beneath and is shared by them all. There are not three Gods. There is only one God, and therefore, in the sense in which we generally use the word, only one person. Yet we cannot say *it* of the Word, for the Word is God in one aspect of His being. We must therefore say, He. And of the Spirit we must say He too, figuratively perhaps, and yet meaning that it is not a mere indefinite afflatus, a literal wind that is breathing on us, but the actual living power of a God who knows and loves. God is one, but in Him there are various activities and powers which, so far as we can know them, are summed up in this threefold name.

This name, therefore, sums up the revelation of God. And, accordingly, it is in—or into—this name that we are baptized. I want to ask, Is it satisfactory? Does it really answer its purpose? The word "name" is equivalent, you know, to manifestation or revelation. Does this name reveal what we most require to know?

That will of course depend on the purpose for which the revelation is required. Is it required to give a complete, an exhaustive, view of the universe? We may easily answer that. No man has, or can have, such a view. The world sees infinite in opposite directions. We cannot know it all. Look at the stars. There they shine above us, "cycles on epicycles, orb on orb." Some of you have read the dream of Jean Paul Richter. The angel takes him from planet to planet, from system to system. He looks in awe-struck wonder at the vast train of innumerable stars. At last he cries in terror, "There *is* no end!" And then the angel answers, "So, also, there is no beginning!" It would be almost the same if we could get microscopes finer and finer still till we had explored the wonders of the world of atoms.

We should never come to an end. The fact is, God is infinite, and He has reflected His own infinity both in the immensely great and in the unspeakably little. No finite mind can grasp the whole. None can know more than a very small fragment of a very small province of the whole. No; the revelation of God's name does not carry us over the wonders of the worlds.

More still : revelation does not satisfy even our possible knowledge and our legitimate curiosity. We know many things not involved in the name of God. This name was revealed in its completeness to the good men of the past. David knew God and loved Him. Paul grasped the mighty thought with rapture, and lived on it and in it. Yet there are boys in our Board Schools who know a hundred things that the saints and sages of the past—Paul and David—never dreamed. As time goes on more and more still will be known. We have powers still to develop. Nay, it is likely that a time may come in the future when all we now know will look like a dot in the vast universe of what will then be known. There may be—I do not know—even faculties of knowledge lying undeveloped in us. Just as some creatures have no eyes or no ears, so we may be without some senses, or other powers of knowing that shall be developed in our remote descendants. But this is not to know the name of God. That is another kind of knowledge; it stands alone. It would not be even desirable that we should be told the details of knowledge. The cause of human development requires that they should be *discovered*, not revealed. But the name of God we must know. It lies at the basis of our character and our hopes.

What, then, is the purpose of the revelation of the name, Father, Son, and Holy Ghost? Its purpose relates to *character*. It is meant to make us good and brave and strong. Yes, and wise too, but with a wisdom that shall affect our feelings and our conduct. It is meant to inspire us, to elevate the whole compass of our thought and emotion, to fill us with the love of man and the joy of God. It comes to develop the whole man, but to do so in the interest of goodness. A man may know much about the stars, he may classify the flowers, he may tell you wonders as to the actions and reactions of the chemical elements, and yet live the life of a fiend or a sensualist. But he who knows the name of God has the knowledge of which it is said, " Ye shall know the truth, and the truth shall make you free," and, " This is eternal life, to know Thee, the only true God," &c. Let us see, then, whether the revelation of the Divine name succeeds in its purpose.

I. It gives us an eternal basis for righteousness and love. This is done by the love of the Father. Why should a man be a good man, just and true,

faithful and pure, loving and gentle? Ask that
question closely, and push it back as far as you
can. You will get many answers. But one only
is satisfactory. You will, *e.g.*, be told, "Goodness will conduce to the man's own happiness."
But suppose he replies, "I do not care for what
you mean by happiness in the future. I am willing to suffer, if need be, so long as I can do as I
please and have my way. A short life, if it must
be so, but a merry one at all cost. Why should I
destroy my youth, or give myself up to your
prudent rules and your sentimental self-sacrifice?"
What can you say to this? You can only say, "If
you will kill yourself, you must; I have no more
to urge." Or, again, you ask, "Why should I be
morally good?" And you get for answer that
rectitude is for the benefit of society taken as a
whole. It would be good for all if each sought
the good of all. No doubt. But why should I
care for the good of all? Why should I give up
my likes and dislikes for another's well-being?
What basis is there in reason for it? especially
as I *may* after all fail to accomplish my purpose.
You will find it difficult to answer such questions
as these. They pose wise heads and earnest
hearts. Sceptics are feeling it all around us.
They see that if Christianity be taken away it will
not be easy to give a convincing *reason* for right
living. I read an article only the other day, ably
written, in which the author says that he sees

quite plainly, unbeliever as he is, that the age
which shall lose Christianity will lose its strongest
motives to live rightly, and to keep the rules of
morality. So say I too. But he does not seem
to see that he is affecting his own argument when
he says so. For he implies that to lose morality,
to lose goodness, is to lose *life*. Man would not be
man if he were not moral. He would be a mere
brute, without reason and without responsibility.

But what does the gospel say to this difficulty? Its
answer is to reveal the Father, and its answer is
explicit and complete. It says, " Be good, for
righteousness is part of the ultimate essence of
the universe. All the laws of nature, and all the
laws of human nature, are founded in it. It is
the law of life to that Infinite and Perfect Being,
of whom all other beings are mere shadows and
phenomena. Man did not invent it. It *was* before
ever the worlds were formed. It is the very
nature of God, and even He cannot change it.
It is above all mere will, for it is an element in
the substance of substances and the cause of
causes. Why should I be true and holy? Ask
the sun why he should shine. Ask the sea why
it should follow the attraction of the moon. Ask
the flower why it should bloom. Righteousness is
the centre, the very core, of all true existence. It
is the inmost being of all men, and to stifle it is
to die. We fight against the ultimate facts if we
do not accept that. All *must* be failure so long as

we stand in opposition to the necessary conditions of life." Yes, duty is ultimate. There is nothing deeper or more essential. It is the life of God, and the only life for man. As Wordsworth says—

> " Stern law-giver, yet dost thou wear
> The Godhead's most benignant grace,
> Nor is there anything more fair
> Than is the smile upon thy face.
> Flowers laugh before thee on their beds,
> And fragrance in thy footing treads,
> Thou dost preserve the stars from wrong,
> And the most ancient heavens through thee are
> fresh and strong."

Or, as the Bible puts it, "Be ye holy, for I (the Father) am holy."

This revelation, then, gives us an eternal basis for righteousness. But it does more. It gives us a reason for love, both special love and love to all men. For it calls God Father, and, observe, it begins with that; it lays the fatherhood of God at the foundation of this very life. He is Father before He is anything else. Now, that is quite invaluable. It shows that the spring of all the doings of God, and the motive power from which the very existence of all other beings flowed is love. God made men, and all other sensitive and rational beings, because He loved them. It seems a paradox, yet it is a truth, that He loved them *before* He made them.* Now two things follow

---

* He thought them into being because He loved them in thought.

from that. First, there is a reason for our love
of each other. If love is from of old, if it is the
pulse-beat of the eternal heart, it is right in us
all. You may love, and I. God cares not only
for those whom we love, but for our love itself;
He approves of it and sympathizes with it.
And then, secondly, love is the strongest power
in the universe. We want a love that is joined
with power. All ordinary love fails us. It passes.
It is either gone from the hearts in which it once
dwelt, so that they who turned to us gladly now
pass us with an averted face, or both the love and
those who felt it are, at least in outward presence,
with us no more. But if God's life is love, *that*
love cannot pass. It is fresh and fragrant now
and for ever. We cannot lose it. Nothing, not
even sin, can destroy it. We can turn to it again
and again. Yes, and in the end love will triumph
too. I puzzle myself very often to understand how
any can doubt that. Surely God is strong. He
is the one and only power into which all others
may be resolved. And if He is love, then love
will conquer. It will destroy sin. It will burn
away all evil from every soul, for our God is a
consuming fire. It will bring home every wanderer. It will bind up every broken heart. It
will open every dungeon door. It will set a crown
of victory on our poverty, our sorrow, our despair.

Turn to this name now—this perfect Fatherhood
of God. Till you do you are lost; you are a poor,

miserable unreality—the mockery, the mere phantasm of your true self. But when you live in the light, and by the power of God, the loving Father, your life is, like His, eternal.

II. This threefold name shows the nobleness and worth of man. Of course I do not now speak of every individual man. This it does by revelation of the Son. I do not speak of any man in his actual present state; but I speak of man as God made him and meant him to be—yes, and still means him to become. Man so regarded is the son of God. In God's eternal thought he has his place. We think of a man's being as though it dated from his birth. But we are wrong. We existed in the thought of God from eternity, for the thoughts of God do not change. Do you not remember how Christ used this fact as an argument for immortality? He tells us that man must live for ever; for the Scripture speaks of God as "the God of Abraham and Isaac and Jacob," and that God "is not the God of the dead, but of the living, for all *to Him* are living." Yes, man—the whole race —past, present, and to come, has now a real life in the thought of God, and has had from eternity. Time is only the way in which we *seem* to ourselves to live. It will one day disappear. We shall awake and see that we exist, and always did, and shall exist in the care and love of God. Christ knew it of Himself. He spoke of the "glory which I had with Thee before the world was."

And it is only because the veil of flesh doth grossly close us in that we do not know it too.

Now, because man is the son of God, he is redeemed. Christ came to unfold the name of the son, which is at once one aspect of the name of God and the proper name of man. Christ is the one only perfect and true man, and therefore He is not merely man, but at the same time " God manifest in the flesh." No ; God did not despise man; how could He when He is Himself the Father of man, and man is made in the likeness of his Father ? When He revealed Himself He did so as a man. You and I despise our humanity. We do not see that God is in it. God is in man, not in spite of His own greatness, but because of it. Most of us want a total revolution in our idea of God. We think God is so great that He has nothing to do with the world. He made it, as a watchmaker makes a watch, and then wound it up and set it going quite apart from Himself. No, indeed no. The old Bible tells a different tale. It does indeed tell us that God is great. It says—" Heaven, even the heaven of heavens, cannot contain thee." But though not contained or enclosed in anything, He fills, penetrates, and sustains everything. God is not shut up in the world. But the world lives, and moves, and is contained in God. The small and the great are both alike to Him, for they are both *in* him. And God is in Christ—*all* of God is there—as all is *everywhere.* Yet He is not *shut up* in Christ. He is so in Christ as thát He is in all who love Him and believe. He is in Christ that He may be in us all, and may give Himself to us all. Christ died for us. The perfect Son of God, our living head, in all things died for us. Did God die, then? Yes, in one sense He did; for Christ in His death expressed the heart of God. It was not a *mere* man that hung upon the cross; it was the "beloved Son" who was one with the Father. But of course God does not *literally* die. It is the finite elements in Christ that do that. The atonement of Christ is the outpouring of the heart of God. It is the price that He pays for our redemption. It is His estimate of the worth of our souls. It is mysterious, wonderful. It is "to the Jews a stumbling-block, and to the Greeks foolishness, but unto us who believe, He is the power of God and the wisdom of God."

Is *that* revelation satisfactory in view of its purpose? Does it bring God to you so that you know and feel His love for you? Can you take Christ—this great power, love, and wisdom of God, as your Saviour and not be pure and holy? I wonder often that any man should for a moment hesitate. This is surely *what* we need, and *all* we need. It fits us like our living skin. It opens to us the fulfilment of all our spiritual wants. It is our strength and our restoration, now and for ever.

III. This name of God—Father, Son, and Holy Ghost—implies such an indwelling of God in man as to make our lives Divine. This is the meaning of the manifestation of the Holy Ghost. The Holy Spirit is God, as He dwells in man. He is not, as I have said, different in metaphysical personality from the Father or the Son. When Christ promises the gift of the Spirit He promises it in all three ways. He says, "*I* will not leave you comfortless ; I will come to you." And, again, after speaking of the Father—"*We* will come to him, and take up our abode with him." And in a third form—"I will send you *another* Comforter," &c. But the thing to notice is, that the Spirit is the indwelling God. We can only speak of the Spirit in figurative terms, and must speak in a personal figure. We cannot say *it* of the Spirit, for there is a real living presence of God to those in whom the Spirit dwells. And why does He come—and come to *stay?* To complete the revelation of God in relation to all our needs. I am in a vast and desolate universe. I fear lest I am orphaned and alone. No ; I am not alone, for the Father is with me. I am conscious of imperfection and wrong-doing. Shall I " cry to the rocks, Fall on me, and to the hills, cover me " ? No ; for the Son appears, taking my nature upon Him, suffering in my suffering, weeping my tears, revealing the pardon and peace of God. I live a poor, little, insipid, worthless life. And then the

Spirit touches me, catches me up like a rushing mighty wind, pours inspiration through all my spiritual being, and fills me with " the power of an endless life."

V

DOUBTS CONCERNING THE SOUL.

"If a man die, shall he live again?"—Job xiv. 14.

THE poet who wrote the Book of Job asked this question, but he had no answer for it—at any rate, no positive answer. He did not know; at best he only dimly and uncertainly hoped. But he did hope. The latter part of the verse implies so much: "All the days," &c. It means, "If I knew that I shall live again, I would wait with perfect patience till that great day." The word translated "change" means a sprouting again; it is applied to the shooting of trees in the spring. It is as though he said, "If I may live again I will not care for the toil of life and its pain. I will wait till my soul blooms forth in leaf and flower and fruit in a nobler world. Everything is bearable if it contributes to an enlarged and ennobled life."

I believe that is a genuine utterance of the heart of man. It speaks your thought and mine

in our real and earnest moments. We long to
live, not to die.

> " Whatever crazy sorrow saith,
>   No life that breathes with living breath
>   Hath ever truly wanted death."

Utter annihilation, blank nothingness, without
thought, without feeling, without will, is a degrading, brutalizing belief to a healthy mind.
If any man seems willing for that, it is a poor
invalid pinched with pain, or a conscience-stricken
one who fears the dreams that may come in the
strange sleep of death. Milton goes so far as to
make even the lost spirits in his picture of the
world of perdition express a horror of sinking into
nothing :

> " For who would lose,
>   Though full of pain, this intellectual being ;
>   These thoughts, that wander through eternity,
>   To perish rather, swallowed up and lost
>   In the wide womb of uncreated night,
>   Devoid of sense and motion ? "

We love the light of day and the sense of
existence. The only worthy termination of life
to us is vaster and fuller life. That is in accordance
with our reason and conscience—in fact, with our
whole nature, and nothing else is.

Why, then, do we hear men speak as though
there were no other life than the earthly life, as
though death were a sleep from which there is

no awaking? Why do we hear them saying that they mean to have " a good time " here, and not even to ask the question whether there be any other life? Partly, I believe, from a real perplexity that springs from an indolent habit of thought. There is nothing most men are less disposed to do than honestly to think things out. They stop at half thoughts and are baffled by the first difficulty. At the first suggestion of doubt they throw the whole problem up in despair. There is another thing also—men do not consider their own nature. They study *things*, cotton, or wheat, or money, if they be business men; rocks, or plants, or animals, if they be scientific; but their own souls they do not study. The world without is read, the world within is a sealed book to them. Let us consider the question of the text, therefore, " If a man die, shall he live again ? " for this is the only doubt, that matters much, concerning the soul.

One reason for thinking that the soul will live hereafter as well as here is, its spiritual nature. What do I mean by that? I mean that it is not a thing which can be measured, weighed, seen, or in any way brought under the cognizance of the senses, like the objects around us, and like our own bodies. It is different from matter, altogether different. It differs by the whole diameter, the entire breadth, of being. Matter is the object seen; the soul is the subject seeing. Matter is the thing touched, examined, described, thought about; the soul is that which feels, investigates, describes, and thinks about it. We know matter by the senses; we know the soul by our own consciousness. I can never know matter as myself—I, the thinking man. I can never know the soul, or at any rate *my* soul, as anything else. It may be true, I think it is true, that even matter resolves itself ultimately into a group of sensations. What I know of it is my own perception of it, and no more, so that, if matter and mind are one at the root, it is far truer to say that matter is a form of mind than to say that mind is a form or an activity of matter. But my point is this—mind and matter are so distinct that we know each chiefly by its distinction from the other. Matter is that in the universe which is not my soul; my soul is that which is over against matter, opposite to it, as the eye is opposite to what it sees. In a word—the world is material, and my soul is spiritual.

And if spiritual, then it need not die with the body. The body dies—it is departed from its mysterious life—becomes cold and still—and then slowly decays into gases, water, and dust, which mingle with the materials around them. But why should the soul die? It is not matter, it has nothing to do with gas, or water, or dust. Why should it not rise out of that wreck? Look at the dead body. Something has gone from it.

Something that was there—aye, and the essential thing—that which gave light to the eye and tune to the voice is there no longer. Where is it? Gone to nothing? What! in a world where every particle of matter is preserved, and every pulse of force is treasured up, can life, love, thought go out and utterly cease to be? Can it? Think of that, I pray you. Is the thing credible? is it after the likeness of what we know in other cases to be true?

Some one may tell me, however, that the soul is an activity of the brain and nerves, as digestion is an activity of the stomach, and circulation of the heart. If the organ perish the activity is gone. But is it so? Am I myself a mere activity of an organ? Not quite, I think. One thing is certain—my organism changes, but *I* remain the same from day to day and from year to year. I know, if I know anything, that I am the same person, the very same and not another, who was once a boy, and afterwards a college student, and then a minister, and who for some years has been preaching and working in this city. But if so, *I* am not an activity of my brain or nerves, very certainly. Men of science tell me that the brain, the nerves, the whole body, change once in every seven years at least, perhaps much oftener. I get a new brain just as certainly though not quite as often as I get a new coat. But men do not change once in seven years! It would be a good thing if

some of them did. They, however, remain the
same. There are memories in this soul of mine
that have been there for several times seven years.
There are pictures on that wonderful *tableau
vivant* of imagination that have remained since
I was almost an infant. Thirty years ago I cut
my head severely and almost bled to death. The
head is not the same, the blood is not the same,
but the ego, the self, the me, is the same and
remembers it extremely well. No, we are not our
nerves or brain, or any part, or property, or
function of our bodies. We are *persons*, with
personal identity, living sameness, from year to
year, and all through the changing circumstances
of a long and eventful life.

Why not, then, after the life which we live in
this world? If we can lay down our body
particle by particle and take up others in the
place of those we part with, why may we not lay
down our body altogether and wake up with
another and nobler body, not material but
celestial? If the gradual change of the body
does not put an end to us, why should the sudden
change of it? Why? I do not know, I cannot
see. My body is not me; why, then, should the
death of my body be the death of me?

We are told that the advance of science is
proving too strong for spiritual theories: they
are to die before it. But what do the chosen
representatives of science say? Mr. Mill tells us

that mind is distinct from body, and, for all he can tell, may exist apart from it. Mr. Bain says the same in almost the same words. Mr. Tyndall says there is an impassable gulf between material and mental processes, and that we have no faculty by which we can pass from one to the other. The fact is that soul and body are not one, but two, closely related no doubt, but not identical. The closest students of them see that the most clearly. If a man tells me that my brain thinks, I answer, No, not my brain, but I. I am not my body, my body is not me. When my body perishes I shall emerge from the ruin, like the bright moth from the chrysalis, and assume a nobler life. " For the trumpet shall sound, and the dead shall be raised incorruptible, and we shall be changed. For this corruptible must put on incorruption, and this mortal must put on immortality. Then shall be brought to pass the saying that is written, Death is swallowed up in victory." These words are sound in philosophy, as well as hopeful in promise. Science has not a syllable to say inconsistent with the glowing splendour of the prospect they disclose.

The deep longing for life which we all feel is another reason for belief in a future life. It is the tendency of every living thing to develop and perfect its life. The flower grows from a mere seed, shapeless and poor, into stem and leaf and glorious blossom. The insect creeps for awhile as

a grub or caterpillar and then bursts into gauzy
wings and a rainbow-coloured life. The wild
creature in the forest rejoices in its strength and
strives to unfold its powers to the utmost. These
live and are satisfied. They want only what they
get, they receive all that their nature can take.
There is no inward unrest, no craving that goes
unsupplied. But it is not so with man. He, too,
grows—the infant becomes a boy, the boy a man,
the man a philosopher, an artist, a statesman, a
saint. But is he satisfied? Does the philosopher
know enough? Has the artist all he wants of
skill or success? Is the statesman as full of
insight and as masterly in policy as he aspires
to be? And the good man, is he not most of all
conscious of imperfection? does he not long for
other and higher things? The law of man's life
is continual growth. Though all the resources of
the world were gathered together and poured out
at the feet of a man, yet would he be conscious
of needs which go beyond natural things and
which only eternity can satisfy. Look at the
poor prodigal. He tries life in every form : wine,
music, brilliant assemblies, the wit of the accomplished, the blandishments of voluptuous beauty,
the splendours which lavish wealth can buy. But
what comes of it all? What can the gilded
and tinselled magnificence of this Vanity Fair of
a world do for a soul, in which eternity is set and
on which the signature of God is written? Can

the law of man's life be fulfilled here? No, no. There are deep longings for a fuller existence in man which can be met and satisfied only in a spiritual world. The intellect has its desires. It longs for truth. It would know—and still know— and continue to gather knowledge till the last riddle is solved and the principles of universal truth lie spread out in sympathy before it. The conscience has its desires. It is unhappy in vice and sin. It longs for purity and goodness. Does it not? Are *you* satisfied with yourself? When you look within and examine your own mental condition, can vice stand that calm look? Does not the lie rankle in your heart after it is told? Do not selfishness and meanness make you blush in secret? Would you not wipe out the pages of your record that are stained with evil? I know you would. And even if you are one who loves God and your fellow-men, do you not long for a purity which you have never reached, and yet which you are never weary of pursuing?

In our best moments we are most dissatisfied. Then most of all we hunger and thirst after a nobler, truer life. Thank God for the words of promise and blessing which fell from the lips of His Divine Son—words which transform this baffled longing into a rainbow of glorious hope: "Blessed are they that hunger and thirst after righteousness, for they shall be filled." The heart, too, has its desires as well as the intellect and the conscience.

Affection is continually disappointed. It is not as pure, as intense, as unselfish as it ought to be and longs to be. Even our noblest love is a sigh for a still better and nobler. We would be purged from the lingering remains of self-regard and taught to love as God loves. Thank God for our love for each other even as it is. Men would be poor wretches if they were not carried out of themselves and knit in affection to those dependent on them. Put a man into solitude and he is a contemptible creature. The holiest words on earth are those that mark our relative condition—such words as father, mother, sister, brother, wife, child. And yet even these are a promise rather than a fulfilment. They are a hint of better things. We must baptize our finite love by contact with an infinite before it grows into all it is capable of becoming. The love of Christ and of the perfect Father must eradicate our love of each other and transform it.

> "Thrice blest whose lives are faithful prayers,
>   Whose loves in higher love endure,
>   What souls possess themselves so pure
> Oh, where is happiness like theirs?"

Now I say that this craving for a higher life is a pledge of immortality. There is a symmetry, an order, in the universe. Things are fitted to one another, and what anything is fit for that it gets. A French thinker says, " our attractions are proportioned to our destinies;" in other words, for every want there is a supply. Is there an eye? There is also light by which it may see. Is there a mind? There is truth fitted to its capacity. Is there love? There are those around us who are its appropriate objects. And as there is in man the idea of a better life and the longing for it, may we not believe, must we not believe, that such a life awaits him? Can we think of the great and good as dead? Is Paul gone to nothingness, or the gentle, loving John, the brave Peter, the holy martyrs? Is the Christ a mere memory, like a beautiful cloud of the morning, that was, and is not? Have the heroes of all the ages, who lifted their own lives and ours above the littleness of time, passed away like a dream? Can the tombs of these men be places where all their thought, goodness, and heroic endeavour lie turned to dust, or are their bodies only there while they themselves have fled beyond the stars? If all other creatures receive according to their nature, shall man, made for immortality, not receive immortality? Shall he stand, the one enigma, the only blot, the solitary contradiction, in this vast and wonderful universe of God? Believe it who will—to me at least it is utterly incredible.

There is a law of development in the universe, too, which seems to imply that if a man die he shall live again. Everything we see is a means to some other and higher thing. The world was

17

once a mere cloud of fiery gas, so scientific men tell us. It cooled a little, and became a fiery liquid. Then it hardened into land, and the vapour condensed into sea. Then came life, very simple at first, but growing more perfect till flowers blushed, trees waved, animals roamed the forest, fishes swam the sea, birds filled the air with music. Some kinds of animals and plants passed away, but always to make room for something better. Then came man. He is better than any animal, for he can think and feel, hope and pray. Man is the end and purpose, the flower and fruit of all. He is self-conscious, and conscious of God; in a word, he is a spiritual being. Will he pass away? If so, it can only be to make room for a still loftier and nobler spiritual being—that is, for man in a higher form. And to what can he pass away? Not, surely, to nothingness. The very fact that he asks these questions proves, or at any rate points to, the answer. As every lower thing is a promise of the life of man, so the conscious, questioning, hoping, fearing life of man is a promise of the hereafter—the fuller development of that life. Do men paint a beautiful picture to tear it in pieces, or build a splendid temple to dash it to the ground? Think what a fully-developed man involves. He is the most costly creature on the earth. Centuries have gone to the making of him. The Bible was written for him. Poets have sung for him. Martyrs have bled to give him liberty and education.

His mother's pain, her tender love, his father's teaching and prayers, moulded his youth. Books, travel, conversation, experience of men and things, sermons, sabbaths, marriage, love, social activities, political and scientific discussion, and a hundred other things have entered into his education. I say such a being is too costly to die like a dog. If he is to die, it is into a larger life. You cannot believe that just when everything is ripened in a man's character—when experience is bearing its richest fruit, when thought is true and feeling noble and conscience pure—death comes in, arrests that magnificent development, and levels that splendid structure with the dust. All things, through boundless past ages, have been leading up to man ; is man, when he comes to be, a meaningless failure, going out into nothingness and night ? Has the mind that planned Raffael's paintings, the mind that sung the " Paradise Lost," the mind that wove the subtle web of Plato's or of Bacon's philosophy simply gone out like the snuff of a candle ? You are a disciple of Mr. Darwin, you say ; you believe in development. Well, I believe in development too, and just because I believe in development, I do not and cannot believe that development ends in nothingness. No, the love of God is the end of development. It begins with simple things, but it ends in a spiritual being that can share the immensity and eternity of God when time and space shall be no more.

We are told sometimes that it is selfish to seek for a future life. We shall die but man will live, it is said, and we ought to be content to live in our descendants, to be immortal in their memory and love. I really cannot see why the desire of life should be a selfish desire. What is selfishness? It is to get my own good at the expense of other people's. The desire of life can only be selfish, then, if my life does harm to other men. But why should it? A good man's life never does. A good man is a benefit, not an injury, to others. The longer he lives and the more widely his influence extends, the better for the world. If that is so in this world, why not hereafter also? Heaven is large enough—we shall not crowd each other out. Nay, every fresh soul admitted to the better world will, as we may well believe, add a new intensity to its joy and a new glory to its triumph. Selfish to desire life beyond the grave! Can I do so much for the good of others, then, if I am blotted out of being? One would imagine that if we are to be a benefit to other men we must at least exist. The Bible speaks of things that are not, bringing to nought things that are, and I can understand that as a vivid figure of speech. But how *men* that are not can do much to improve the condition of men that are is a puzzle that I cannot comprehend.

One thing, however, we may wisely learn from objections such as these: to keep our idea of the

better life large and noble. Some people's notion
of heaven is poor, narrow, and selfish enough.
They fancy that there every wish will be gratified,
and the condition of others will give them no concern. I do not believe it. It seems to me utterly
preposterous and impossible. We shall have something better to do than to sit on a cloud and sing.
We shall not spend eternity in wandering through
scented groves or plucking golden fruit. I can
believe that there will not only be unselfish love,
but even voluntary self-sacrifice in the better
world. God is there, who is eternal love and
perfect righteousness. Christ is there, who bore
the bitter cross for our salvation. God and Christ
do not change; they are the same yesterday and
to-day and for ever. If we are to share their
heaven we must be like them. And there may,
for anything we know, be abundant room for
mutual help and mutual sacrifice. We shall not
be all alike. And as long as one has what another
has not, whether knowledge, or goodness, or peace,
or power, there will be opportunity, just as in this
world, for one to help and to bless another. Oh,
men and women, do not shrink from that! for
the sacrifices of love are perfect bliss. In heaven,
as on earth, "it is more blessed to give than to
receive."

It is an evidence also that we shall live again,
that the belief in a future life is intertwined with
all religions. However widely separated in time cr

place, all who worship in any way have some hope and belief in a life to come. These universal beliefs of the human mind are to be regarded, I cannot help thinking, with very deep respect. The great human soul does not utter itself idly or carelessly. An old proverb says, "The voice of the people is the voice of God." The "people" there are not a chance mob collected at the corner of a street, but the mighty masses of the human race. The universal consent of the race is strong evidence for anything. You cannot prove most fundamental truths; they go before proof, so to say, they are too simple to be proved. Why do we believe that there is an outward world? that this church, and I who speak, and you who hear, are not dreams but realities? We can never prove these things to one another. Yet we never doubt them. It is not common sense to doubt them, we say. Exactly so. The sense of truth which is common to all men, the net result, as I may call it, of all man's thought and experience is on the side of these great truths. So of the being of God. The Bible assumes it as not needing proof. So of a soul destined to live hereafter. It is not so much asserted as implied in all Scripture, and, indeed, in all religion. Even the Indian has his happy hunting-grounds for the good warrior after death. The Buddhist has his blissful Nirvana—a rest in the bosom of the first cause. The mystic has his vision of God. The Christian has his heaven.

To this question, then, " If a man die, shall he live again ? " the great human heart answers Yes. And Christ, who is the great human heart purified and made perfect by the indwelling of God, answers Yes too. He knew what was in man, for He *was* man, expanded and ennobled into divinity. And it was said of Him, " Thou wilt not leave His soul in Hades, neither wilt Thou suffer thine Holy One to see corruption."

This horrible, deadening, benumbing nightmare, the dread of annihilation, received its deathblow when Christ arose. " Now is Christ risen from the dead, and become the firstfruits of them that slept. For as in Adam all die, even so in Christ shall all be made alive. O grave, where is thy victory ? O death, where is thy sting ? Thanks be to God, who giveth us the victory through our Lord Jesus Christ."

What then ? The lesson is simple : live as immortal souls ; be worthy of "honour, glory, and immortality—eternal life." We may be so. Not in ourselves, for we are at the best unprofitable servants, and when not at our best we are defiled and stained by dreadful forms of sin. But we may rise through Christ into newness of life. The very worst of us may be washed, may be renewed, may be sanctified. Whether we will or no, we are acting and thinking for eternity. We live, and we *must* live, for ever. What shall that life be ? It will be what we make it. It will grow out of the present life, as the flower grows out of the root, as our manhood grows out of childhood and youth. The other world is only this world expanded and prolonged. Properly speaking, there is only one world, one order, one system of law and Divine government. This is the first half, the second is beyond the grave. And as surely as what we are to-day has grown out of what we were yesterday and the day before, so surely will our life hereafter be determined by our life here.

VI

THE CHARACTER OF CHRIST—IS IT DIVINE?

"And the Word was made flesh and dwelt among us."
—John i. 14.

CHRIST, we are told, is the Word of God made flesh. It is a very strange phrase, but it is full of meaning. A word is an uttered thought. It is a thought which has found for itself expression. Christ is the thought of God uttered or expressed. Very wonderful it is that thought can be expressed in words. Words are sounds only, vibrations of the air, little waves in the atmosphere around us. But inwardly they are quite different. Their body, so to speak, is air in movement, but their soul is a thought or feeling in some human heart. And they have the power of kindling thought in the hearts of others similar to that in the mind which uttered them. They are living messengers, swift winged, and nimble footed, flying between souls. Very wonderful, if you think of it. I have a thought in my mind. I strike with my lips or my tongue upon the air, and instantly the same thought is in yours. In that way we can play upon each other's minds as a musician plays upon an organ. We can awaken thought or imagination, anger or rage, hope or love. The power of speech is the bond of society. It makes the difference between a herd of animals and a society of men. By speech minds mingle and unite. Man's word is man's bond of brotherhood. And God's Word is God's thought and feeling expressed. The text says they are expressed not in sounds, but in a human life. No soul could reveal the heart of God. It required all that Christ was and is to do that. God's love is infinite, and it could only find expression in the boundless goodness and love of the Saviour. For there is something infinite in Christ. We all feel that. You look and look, you listen, you take all you can, but still there is something more. As one has said, "There is an unknown quantity in Christ." Whatever you know, there is more to be known. He is higher than thought can rise and deeper than thought can fathom. Paul spoke what we all feel when he wrote of "the unsearchable riches of Christ."   And that boundless spiritual wealth— that fulness of wisdom and love is there because He is the Word made flesh, the expression of the very heart and life of God. He is the gateway leading into the fulness of the Divine nature.

Now I am not going to attempt any answer to the question how the Divine and human are united in Christ. Other men may know, or think they know; I frankly confess I do not. But that Christ is Divine I fully and heartily believe. I cannot tell you now half my reasons. But taking His character in the most external way, I can point out to you a few qualities that startle us into the thought that He must be more than man.

I. Look at the purity of His life. As a fact I assume that. Here is One who is "holy, harmless, undefiled, and separate from sinners." He Himself says, "Which of you convinceth Me of sin?" and there is no reply to His question. It is the impression He actually made on men that He was sinless. How wonderful, when the most certain and universal of all facts is the sinfulness of mankind! Everybody feels it. Only folly or utter baseness can be insensible to it. The man who said he had no sin would take the shortest way of proving that he was a sinner. We feel our sinfulness just in proportion as we rise above it, the best men feel it most. The saints of all ages are those who have made the very air ring with cries and groans over their selfishness and impurity and hardness of heart. But here is One who dwells in an atmosphere of pure devotion, who is as simple as a child, and as gentle as a lamb, who is so close to God that when other men are sleeping He spends whole nights in prayer, and yet He never betrays by word or look the faintest consciousness of sin. Once in the history of the world there has been a sinless life. Once Divine purity has touched the earth, and acted, spoken, and lived among men.

The very idea of a sinless life is one which we get from the gospel. Moses is not sinless. David is not; the Psalms are resonant with his passionate confessions of sin. Paul is not sinless; he calls himself "the chief of sinners." The same is true outside the Bible. The founders of other forms of religion, such men as Menu in India, Mahomet in Arabia, Confucius in China, and whatever others we may take, do not claim to be sinless or perfect, and their followers do not claim it for them. On the contrary, whole pages are taken up with the story of their mortifications and penances for sin. But Christ never even asks to be forgiven. He knows and feels that He is utterly accepted already, completely at one with God. "As Thou, Father, art in Me and I in Thee"—that is the way in which He speaks of Himself. Oh, blessed and sacred life! the world is a different place since it was lived among men. May its gentle and glorious power descend upon us!

Take notice, too, that the character of Christ cannot be a dream. It must be real. Do you say that the Evangelists invented it? Never. Who were the Evangelists? Men of no skill in writing, very simple and unconventional. They could not have described a perfect life through two pages if they had not drawn from nature. If you doubt what I say, try what you can do. Write the life of a perfect man and see what you will make of it. I can tell you beforehand: he will either be covered with faults and follies, or he will be a mere milksop. But the Christ of the Gospels is neither. His goodness is glorious, positive goodness. It is not the mere absence of faults, it is full of the most inspiring excellencies. It is not the pale glimmer of the moonlight, cold as an icicle, it is the glow and warmth, as well as the splendour of the sun. What element of human greatness is absent? Do you speak of courage? Here is One who calmly faces an enraged nation, and stands unmoved amid the howling opposition of a bigot priesthood and an angry crowd. Or is it benefi-cence you would see? Surely it is here, for it is true of Him that "He went about doing good." Self-sacrifice is a noble thing, is it? Where, then, will you find a sacrifice equal to His who gave up all the comforts of home and love so that "He had not where to lay His head," and at last per-mitted the folly and the sin of man to tear His gentle heart in pieces? And then, how He knew men! how He understood them with the keen insight of love! how He saw them through and through, so that every thought and emotion lay open to His eye! "Come, see a man that told me all things that ever I did," said the woman of Samaria, and she added, with better reason than she fully under-stood, "Is not this the Christ?" Yes, friends, it is the Christ! It is He "who loved us, and washed us from our sins in His own blood." He knows us because He loves us, for only love can see the contents of another soul. Poor as we were, weak and wayward, He loved us. He thought, not of what we were, but of what we might become. He picked our souls out of the dark cavern of evil that they might shine as jewels on the brow of God for ever. "He loved us foul that He might make us fair," as St. Augustine so tenderly says. He saw the glorious possibilities of our soiled and degraded nature—the ideal that lay buried and embruted in our miserable life, and He gave Himself to pain and even to death that He might rescue it from destruction and restore it to goodness and to God. Men and women, He did this for you! And He asks in return only one thing—that you will love Him, and the Father whom He reveals, with all your ransomed nature.

A goodness and purity like this of Christ seems to me Divine. If this is not a mark of the presence of God I do not know what could be. I accept Christ, therefore, as the Son of God and the Saviour of men. I say, "Lord, I come to Thee, Thou hast the words of eternal life."

II. The greatness of the love of Christ, and especially its broad comprehensive inclusiveness, seems to me Divine. Intense love is always a noble thing. Even in the humblest creatures it is a sort of element or promise of nobility. The love of a faithful dog for his master makes the dog almost

human for the time. It leads us to look even on
the animal nature with something of respect and
reverence. And the love of mothers for children,
fatherly love, sisterly and brotherly love, the love
of husband and wife—all the love, in a word, for
which home is the symbol, how precious and how
sacred they are! They are the tender and heavenly
oases in our life, otherwise so prosaic and common.
They make us hope for fuller love hereafter, they
enable us to believe in heaven, and render God
credible. When love grows less personal and more
general, it is more inspiring, if not so tender and
consoling. The love of a patriot for his country
stirs every heart and kindles our warm admiration.
King Alfred in England, Robert Bruce in Scotland,
William Tell in Switzerland—their very names are
words to move enthusiasm. But love as a rule goes
no further than love of country. The love of man
as man is not common. Certainly it was not in
the ancient world. Love is apt to grow weaker
and thinner the more it is widened out: you
cannot love a million people as you can love one.
But Christ loved all men. He looked into every
human face and said, " brother." He spoke to the
Samaritan woman—an alien and a heretic—and
said, " sister." He gave us a prayer, not for you
or me, but for all men, and its first words are,
" Our Father." Poor slaves at their tasks, little
children at school, ragged outcasts, the mere waifs
and strays of society—He taught them all to say,

" Our Father." This came to Him out of His own
Divine heart, and out of that alone. Where else
could He find it ? Certainly not among his country-
men, the Jews. Of all people on earth they were
the most intensely narrow and national. They were
the people of God, and all others were mere "dogs,"
to be hated and despised. Even now their descendants keep themselves sternly separate from all
other races. They are scattered all over the world.
You may see their well-known features—the dark
eye and the aquiline nose—wherever men gather
for business, and wherever there is money to be
made. They are a patient, thrifty, earnest, successful race of men. But they are separate—" among
us, but not of us." Think of it : Christ sprang of
that intense people, ready to die for its special
privileges, and yet He opened His mighty heart so
as to embrace all humanity, and preached a gospel
to every clime and colour, to every race and
condition of mankind. It is not wonderful that
we should care for the human race. We have had
Christ to teach us. His cross is the symbol and
the means of reconciliation. Paul, His truest
disciple in this respect at all events, delighted to
call himself " the apostle of the Gentiles "—that is,
not of the Jews only, but of all mankind. Even
Peter, whose mind opened much more slowly to
new truths than Paul's, grew to see that he should
not call any man common or unclean.

For eighteen centuries we have heard the grand

truth that men are brothers for Christ's sake. And modern science and discovery are helping the good work on. The telegraph binds the two hemispheres of the world together. The steamship throbs on the bosom of every sea. The bounds of the nations are growing unsettled and the families of man are melting into one. The gospel is proving itself adapted to every nation as well as every moral and spiritual state. It is the only religion that can get beyond national bounds. Mahomedanism is for the East alone; it will not flourish under a northern or western sky. Menu is read and understood in India, and India only. Buddhism cannot get out of China and Japan. But Christ goes everywhere. He is at home in every civilization and under every sky. The tropics open to him their sunny groves, warm with the breath of a thousand spices; the western prairie unrolls its broad bosom to receive Him, and waves its plains of feathery grass in welcome; the frozen Pole unlocks its icy fetters and thaws into genial warmth at His approach. Come, Thou great King of Saints, assume Thy power and reign, the voice of blending humanity calls Thee, and all creatures sigh to be redeemed.

III. We get another mark of the Divine character of Christ in the unselfishness of His devotion to the great purpose of His life and work. It is very notable that Christ is never thinking of Himself. He lives for His Father and for men. This unselfishness is

18

a wonderful mark of His divinity. God, you know, is the only Being in the universe who can receive nothing. He gives continually; He is the great Giver; but He does not receive, for He has all things already. We speak of giving to God, but what we so give is really set apart in His name for the good of our fellow-men. There is one exception, indeed— God longs for our *love*, and we can give that to Him. But of outward things we can give Him nothing. Christ has this peculiarity of the Divine character —He is always giving, never receiving. When He went up to Jerusalem as a boy He employed Himself about His Father's business. In manhood His one thought was to do the will of God and to work out the good of man. He wandered from end to end of His native country that He might find those who needed Him most and who were able to receive benefit from Him. Twelve men joined Him as disciples. He taught them and cared for them, loved them and cherished them as a mother devotes herself to her children. He adapted Himself to their different temperaments, bore with the treacherous Judas, restrained the impetuous Peter, confirmed the sceptical Thomas, guided the aspiring John. His mighty works also were works of unselfish love. His own description of them is proof of that—" the blind see, the deaf hear, the lame walk, the dead are raised, to the poor the gospel is preached." And His teaching is full of the same spirit. It is full of the idea of love, nothing for

self and all for others. The idea of love to God
and His fellow-men haunts Him like a passion; He
cannot for a moment tear Himself away from it.
Even when He asserts Himself it is for the sake of
others. "I am the Way, and the Truth, and the
Life," He says; but He says it that He may go on
to invite storm-tossed and sinful men to receive
truth and life from Him. And I need not surely
speak of His death, when "He made His soul an
offering for sin," and bowed His head to endure
"the contradiction of sinners against Himself."
There is a steady consistency of self-sacrifice in it
all. One great act of self-devotion is not uncommon
among us. Thank God, even in our imperfection
some germs of heroism are left. But it is not one
great act that is difficult, it is the thousand little
acts of daily life. It is to keep true, and keep on
under all circumstances, that tries the character.
Many a man would jump into the fire to rescue his
burning wife who hurts and tortures her feeling
almost every day. Many a woman would die for
her husband, who yet teases him past endurance
by a complaining or scolding tongue. Where is he
who is consistent in self-devotion? I know of none
but Christ. And this complete sacrifice of self is
the divinest thing in the universe. It is of God
and it leads to God. It is the very essence of the
Divine life. The Christ who had it is not man
merely but "God manifest in the flesh."

IV. Another of the marks of a Divine character

in Christ is the calmness of His faith in His own
work and mission. Christ believed in Himself.
He had no doubt of the divinity of His own life and
work. Of course, taken alone, that proves nothing.
Many fanatics have believed in themselves; but it
is not possible to think of Christ as a fanatic. He
was too wise, too good, too reasonable. He won all
hearts by His wisdom and goodness. And He said
in all quietness and firmness that God had sent
Him, and that He was the Son of God. He declared
that He was the Saviour of mankind, of whom
prophets and psalmists had spoken, and encouraged
all men to come to Him for peace and spiritual life.
He believed that the course of the world's history
was guided so as to secure the ultimate triumph of
the gospel. He said that He, if He were lifted up,
would draw all men unto Him. He had perfect
faith in God and truth and goodness. And He
had no doubt that goodness and truth for men were
bound up with His own work. He believed in the
future. He did not despair of the destiny of the
race. He was not one of the gloomy prophets who
are for ever saying that the world is going to
rack and ruin. No, no; Christ saw that truth is
stronger than falsehood, right is mightier than
wrong, love is greater than malice. A day is coming
when the right and the true will conquer. The
world is in course of development, of evolution, of
progress, and some day "right—reason, and the
will of God—will prevail." So Christ died, knowing

that not only He but His glorious Gospel would rise again from the dead and live for evermore.

And it will be so. The Gospel of Christ is invincible. No power of earth or hell can conquer it. His cause is the cause of God, and of man, and all things fight for it, even those that seem at first sight to threaten it. As one of His own disciples tells us, speaking in the very spirit of his blessed Master, "We can do nothing against the truth, but for the truth." Unbelief, opposition, persecution, are only making the success of the truth of God more sure. "He maketh the wrath of man to praise Him, and the remainder of wrath He will restrain."

Brethren, I ask you to weigh these things. Is Christ Divine? Is He the Son of God and the Saviour of men? Did He die for you and for me? Did He care so much for our spiritual life as to bear the cross that He might secure it? Did He lie in the tomb that we might not be lonely there, but feel Him with us in death as well as in life? Then what are we doing in response to His mighty love? Have we taken Him for our friend and Saviour, the guiding star of our pilgrimage, and the haven of our rest? Let us do it, and do it now. Life is short and uncertain. The pageants will soon be over and the lights will be put out. It will not matter then whether we were wealthy or wise, or what figure we made in society. But it will matter infinitely what we *are*. And it is only Christ who can take us in our weakness and sin and make us what we ought to be.

VII

HIS GLORIOUS BODY.*

"Who shall change our vile body, that it may be fashioned like unto His glorious body, according to the working whereby He is able even to subdue all things unto Himself."—PHIL. iii. 21 (*A. V.*).

"Who shall fashion anew the body of our humiliation, that it may be conformed to the body of His glory, according to the working whereby He is able even to subject all things to Himself."—PHIL. iii. 21 (*R. V.*).

THE better translation is that of the Revised Version. We are told that as Archbishop Whately lay on his death-bed his chaplain read to him this chapter. "Yes," said the dying man; "but read again, and translate literally, for nothing that He made is vile." And that is true. Our body is not vile, "cheap," or "common," as the old word implied; it is fearfully and wonderfully made, a mystery of Divine wisdom and skill. And yet it is rightly called "the body of our humiliation," for it is often the seat of disease and pain,

* The last sermon. Preached in Brixton Independent Church on Easter Sunday evening, April 6, 1890.

and always, at least to some degree, a hindrance to our noblest life. Its clamorous appetites load the wings of our aspirations as though with lead, and occupy so much of our thought and attention that we have little to spare for the affections that bind us to each other, and the truth that unites us to God. No doubt the bodily senses are inlets of various knowledge. All we know of the universe around us comes through one or other of these five gateways. But we have reason to believe that there are many facts even in the material world of which they do *not* tell us; and they give us no knowledge at all of the world of spiritual realities. They say nothing of God, of Christ, of the unseen regions in which those whom we have loved are living; and of the eternal truth and goodness which are the proper food of our souls. We cannot boast much of our body. It is at best only the beginning of something better. It ties us to one place. It holds us too much to its own service. It is seldom, at least in the majority of men, in very good condition. It is apt to intrude on us with its aches and pains. It is not often, even in outward appearance, perfectly noble in men or perfectly beautiful in women. And yet, as the good Archbishop said, it is not " vile." We cannot afford to despise it. Even in the outward form of it there is something that takes us in thought beyond itself. Its upright attitude expresses something of the dignity of the soul which uses its activities. Its features are animated with thought and feeling. The eye, the lip, the pale or blushing cheek, the smile, the knitted brow, are all a picture language that sometimes speaks more than words. Though mortal, the body is symbolical. Though material, it partakes something of the character of spirit. It seems to stand on the border line between the worlds of matter and mind, itself doomed to death, and yet promising immortality to the guest who inhabits it.

Perhaps under the outward body which we see there is something more; what we may call an inward body, or the germ of one, invisible to us now, but preparing to become visible in the next world. St. Paul speaks of a "spiritual body." Is that forming, so to speak, as a sort of kernel within the shell of the natural body? Is it the reality of which the present body is only the appearance? Is there, within the grosser flesh and blood, a body related more blessedly to the ascended body of Christ, a house of the soul which may be truly called "a building of God, a house not made with hands, eternal in the heavens"?

"His glorious body," says our text. He has, then, a glorious body. The words carry us back in thought to the resurrection morning. The body of Christ, if we may trust the Scriptures, came, then, out of the tomb. If it was the body which had been laid in the grave three days before, it was that body with a difference. A change, a very

great change, had passed upon it. It was no
longer the weak, frail body that had not where to
lay its head. It was now a body elevated above
ordinary conditions, and, so to speak, spiritualized.
The proofs of this are quite clear if we follow the
narrative. The disciples are told to go to Galilee,
and, when they arrive there, they will find that He
is there "before" them. How did He go? Along
what road, or by what means of transit? All we
know is that, when they arrived, He was *there*,
ready to reveal Himself to them. It seems as
though the risen body of Christ had the power of
passing over space at will, or of making itself
visible in different places, without passing over the
space between them. When the two disciples
were walking together, on the way to Emmaus, the
risen Jesus suddenly joined them, and, after His
conversation with them, as suddenly vanished out
of their sight. They did not know till afterwards
who it was, though their "hearts burned within
them when He talked with them by the way, and
when He opened to them the Scriptures." So
again He came into the midst of the disciples
where they were assembled together, "the doors
being shut." No walls or doors could shut out the
risen body of the Lord; it was so one with His
Spirit that it came and went exactly as He willed.
It is true there seems to have been some sort of
material quality still belonging to it. Christ says
that it is not merely the apparition of His Spirit,

for " a spirit hath not flesh and bones as ye see Me have." Christ's risen body seems to belong to *both* the material and spiritual worlds, and to connect them together. It was the same as it always had been, yet different. At last, on the ascension day, Christ took His disciples apart, and was taken up into heaven, and a cloud received Him out of their sight. Then He entered the spiritual world, and was no more seen on earth. What of bodily medium He took thither was no longer flesh. It was His " glorious body" now. We cannot tell what it is, except that it serves, as our own body does, as a means of making Him manifest to other spirits around Him. We shall *know* Him— we who have loved and followed Him. He will be directly revealed in the " body of His glory." Yes, blessed Lord, we too shall be allowed to recognize Thee for whom our souls have longed !

Notice that the " glorious body" of Christ involves His perfect humanity. It is the form or shape of the perfect man. And it is also the form in which God is revealed. There, as here, the blessed One with whom our life is identified is at once God clothed with humanity and man elevated into deity. The indwelling God beams from the eyes, speaks from the lips, is manifest in the acts of Christ. In His own being God transcends form, for He is infinite, but in so far as He is expressed in form it is in the glorified humanity of His Son. It would seem that there is something in the human form which is fitted to be the expression of God. Man's shape is akin to his soul, and his soul is akin to God. So that the perfect man is, in order to be perfect, more than a man. His finiteness shades off into the infinite, His humanity trembles into deity. God to be manifested must become a man, man when he is perfected is one with God. Here, then, let us seek and find our God—in Jesus, whom we see and know. He speaks to us, not in the thunder or in the stormy sea; we hear a *man's* voice, a voice like our own, full of sympathy with our sorrow, pity for our pain, forgiving love stronger than all our sin. He comes to meet our sin and to break its dreadful power. He stands by us to suffer at our side. He takes our death upon Him, and through death "conquers him that has the power of death." He is here to pour Himself into our life—Himself the conquering man, Himself the compassionate God. Think of this in your hours of darkness and depression. You are apt to feel as though one so poor and mean could not be an object of care to a being so august as God. But it is one like you— poor, rejected, despondent, despised and crucified of men, who is elevated to the throne of power, and who will change the body of your humiliation as He has that of His own.

The glorious body of Christ involves also His *universal presence.* The ascended Saviour is freed from the limits of time and place. He is not con-

fined, as He was in the days of His flesh, to one
spot, so as to be absent from other places because
He is present in that. The body of His glory,
whatever else it may be, is absolutely obedient to
the uses of His Spirit. It is here, it is there, it is
yonder, wherever He wills. We may rightly think
of Christ, therefore, as present with us always and
everywhere. I do not attempt to explain that. I
cannot tell you how the spiritual body of Christ
can be in many places at the same time ; but we
may get a glimpse of what is meant when I remind
you that *God* can be everywhere at once. This,
too, not partially but wholly. It is not that a
fragment of the Godhead is here and another
there, but the whole of Him, His infinite love, His
perfect wisdom, His boundless power, is equally
present to every part of the entire universe. We
never can be where He is not. And what is true
of God is true of Christ. Christ is present everywhere, and the whole Christ, too, so that we may
enjoy all the fulness of what He is and what He
has to give. Invisible He is, no doubt, and must
be so until we acquire the powers which enable us
to perceive His glorious body ; but He is not absent
because He is invisible. The powers most important in moulding our lives are often invisible ;
so is Christ. In our hours of prayer He is near,
kindling our emotion and guiding our thought.
In the thrill of joy over a vanquished sin, or new
impulse toward God and goodness, we may recog-

nize His presence. In the stir and stress of puzzling business life, some gentle thought, some sudden perception of what it is right to do, some clearing away of temptation to follow a base motive, or descend to an unworthy act of fraud or chicanery, will reveal the presence and the inspiration of our Lord. In pain, too, we shall find Him at hand, for He knows the keen misery of pain and the sense of desertion it is so apt to bring. And at the last hour, when the damps of death gather on our brow, we may expect the presence and the love of Christ to soothe us and to speak a word of peace as we go out on the great unknown ocean that lies beyond our life. The whole of our life may be penetrated with the presence of Christ. He is the perfection of all human nobleness, and the power of His presence *must* ennoble us. The touch of Christ, like the alembic of the alchemist, turns even the basest metal into gold.

Christ " shall change the body of our humiliation," says the text, so that it shall " be fashioned like unto the body of His glory." Out of our common, earthy life, He will make a glorious heavenly one. This suggests one view of the very meaning of our present life. We are in all our experience laying up the materials for that change. We are preparing to be made in the image of Christ. What value that may give even to the apparent trifles of our experience! You forget a thousand things, but they do not forget *you.* All your past leaves its mark on your character. It leaves you different from what it found you. The lessons you learned in your youth as you sat in school, or were drilled for your present work, are most of them forgotten in detail. But they have left their impress on your mind; they have educated you. You are wholly different from what you would have been *without* them. This is true of our spiritual experience also. Take our sorrows, for example. They come to us, and very mysterious they seem. They pass away, and somehow we find ourselves wiser. We cannot tell how the wisdom came, but it is *there.* The sins that we first loved, then hated, and finally, with a great struggle, forsook, have taught us more than we could have learned in any other way. The same is true of our hours of prayer and aspiration—they are with us still. All our sympathy and love for others, all our acts of unknown kindness, the dear faces that we left behind us in the past—all these lie in us like germs waiting for the change. They will show their effects in that renewed character which finds its outward expression in the glorious body. There is no loss. Good will spring from every good deed and thought. You ask, What will our glorious body be? Well, I do not know. But it will be appropriate to *us.* "To every seed its own body." Our heavenly embodiment corresponds exactly to our character; it expresses precisely what we *are.*

We are building it now. Or, if not a heavenly, then we are preparing an embodiment suited to our evil character—we are making ready our perdition. The glorious body is in contrast not only with our present earthly body, but with one of a spiritual quality fitted to those who choose corruption and death. The change will not alter character; it will bring out and exhibit the character that is *there*. The fire does not write the letters in invisible ink, it only manifests what has been already written. I have seen a picture in the space of a pin's point. To the naked eye it was *not* a picture, only a faint, dark spot, but under the microscope it unfolded into vastness and robed itself in beauty. So is it with the future of our souls. It is the present enlarged to its full proportions, developed to its ultimate results. Take care, then, what the present is. And the best care you can take is to place it in the hands of Him who can take out of it all that is evil and wrong, and fashion it first in spirit, and then in form, like unto His own beauty and glory.

[The following article written by Dr. Stevenson on the death of Dr. Elmslie has been thought in many respects singularly descriptive of himself. It is therefore inserted in this volume.]

PROFESSOR ELMSLIE, D.D.

THE stroke of Professor Elmslie's death will be to many simply overwhelming. So much came to them in him, and so much has been wrenched from them, that the sense of loss will be akin to misery. What we of the Christian Church especially want at present is a band of men, young in vigour, ripe in scholarship, scientific in sympathy and method, thoroughly at home in Biblical research, and with all these qualities, simple in piety and unshaken in faith. These advantages are not common, even apart from each other, but united in a fascinating harmony, they are as rare as they are noble. Yet they dwelt in ripening perfection in Dr. Elmslie. He stood as one of the select band who are making sacred literature scientific, so as to reclaim for theology and twine around her brow the chaplet of her intermitted queenship. It seemed, some years ago, as though physical science were about to supersede theological inquiries. A disposition showed itself on the part of theologians to resist these scientific claims. But the terrible advancing power came on, threatening to paralyse our loftiest hopes. Meanwhile a number of brave men, both here and on the Continent, were adopting the methods of science and applying them in Biblical inquiry. Almost as soon as they began to do so, light seemed to break. We saw the revelation of God in the process of its growth, and became more sure of its divinity than ever. Of this school of reverent, fearless inquirers Professor Elmslie was first a pupil and then a teacher. And as we listened to his results, achieved by "mild enthusiasm," and declared with the clearness of crystal, we became conscious that the Bible was a larger gift than most men had hitherto dreamed, and destined to hold its own for ever in the religious consciousness of man.

Of course Professor Elmslie did not stand alone. But he had gifts which make it especially trying to lose him. He was not only learned, he had the rare power of self-conveyance. He could induce in others the love of knowledge, the keen hunting instinct by which he was himself inspired. Fragments of Scripture history, as he touched them, glittered with fascination like diamonds. Names and dates ceased to be dry and became full of significance. The glow of his expressive eye, the tentative effort of his voice, the final burst of brilliant words kept attention untiringly on the stretch. He was your fellow-student, ahead of you, perhaps, but still near your side. His tone of quiet, modest confidence, too, was greatly charming. As he developed the results of study you felt yourself in the presence of one who knew. Here was a man to whom the facts of the Bible were like those of geology to Lyell, or those of astronomy to Lockyer or Stewart. Flashes of unexpected side-light kept kindling delighted interest and bringing the distant near. Of one thing we who listened to him were sure : whatever might be the ultimate results, this was the sound and satisfactory method of research. We were face to face with facts, and they were speaking for themselves.

Professor Elmslie had, as part of his equipment, a fine appreciation of historical character. It was this that rendered his sermons and lectures on the heroes of Old or New Testament story so fresh and powerful. We had read the facts before, but only as they passed through his mind did they serve to reveal the play of motive and purpose, of thought and feeling, which lay behind them. Ancient days and manners he could make alive again. He had something of the power, which is so signally displayed in Robertson, to nestle into the hearts of the men of old, stand where they stood, think as they thought. His learning, so far from hindering, helped him in this. It added dramatic picturesqueness to his sympathetic insight, so that his descriptions stood out in relief as though carved on a gem. He could gently loosen the bonds of time and place, of here and now, so bringing us into contact with those principles of humanity which are always the same. Very natural did the heroes of the Scripture seem as he spoke of them, while yet they did not lose a jot of the undying significance which constitutes their speciality as entering into Divine revelation. They were men and women to the finger-tips, yet they were representative as well as individual.

There was also, in the preaching of Professor Elmslie, a very high form of what we mean by the practical element. Dr. Arnold defined practical Christianity as " great thoughts underlying small duties." There was no shrinking in the preaching of Dr. Elmslie from an insistence on the minutest details of duty. They were indicated, enforced, tellingly described. But not for a moment were his auditors allowed to lose sight of the great principles, without which exhortations to duty are likely to become so weary. We have seen sometimes the web which a spider has woven, loaded at intervals with drops of morning dew. Suddenly the sun has shone forth and every drop has become a jewel, brilliantly sparkling. The duties of life, colourless in themselves, were lighted up in the expositions of Dr. Elmslie with a similar radiance, because seen in relation to far-reaching and permanent principles.

The doctrinal teaching of Professor Elmslie was comprehensive and rich.   He was not satisfied with a partial or merely logical view of any of the great doctrines of the Gospel.   He delighted to look at them from different sides, and to set them in various points of light.   His teaching was eminently constructive.   There was no tendency in his mind to rejection for the sake of novelty or change.   He was probably more keenly alive to the presence of truth under varied forms than eager to overthrow any mode of thought which has ever yielded nourishment to the spiritual life of earnest and godly men.   Hence he was popular with men of different mental tendencies, although entirely candid and fearlessly outspoken.   Attached deeply and sincerely to the Church to which he belonged, breathing in the atmosphere of her noblest spirit as well as accepting the letter of her formularies, he looked forward to the advent of fuller light and vaster truth as the result of wider investigation.   He did not expect to destroy or even innovate, but perpetually to add ; and saw in the theology he loved so well the grandest gymnastic of the human mind, as well as a majestic vestibule to the temple of God.

We can ill spare such men.   The times need them.   We cannot live to-day on the thoughts of the past except as they are quickened and verified by comparison with the whole sphere of the completest knowledge.   The religious truth which will feed us must fall into harmonious relations with our large, intense, many-sided experience. The sciences of nature, of man, and of society cry out for an adequate conception of theology as their crown and topstone; and the battle of life, growing continually more strenuous, can only be fought successfully in the power of a comprehensive faith in Christ. Professor Elmslie was the man to appreciate the situation, and to prepare others to undertake it. Why he has been taken from us must remain a mystery. To the college which has lost him we can only offer our sincerest condolence. With the Church of which he was an ornament we cherish the truest sympathy. The deeper grief of the bereaved family is too sacred for more than the most respectful allusion. We trust that the mantle of his ripe scholarship, his genial piety, and his noble enthusiasm may fall on many, especially on his former pupils, and quicken them to a like intensity of endeavour and fulness of self-devotion.

The Gresham Press,

UNWIN BROTHERS,

CHILWORTH AND LONDON.

JAMES CLARKE & CO.'S BOOKS.

Pamphlets.

THE BEAUTY OF GOD, AND OTHER SERMONS. By T. VINCENT TYMMS. Price 2d. 12s. per 100.

AN APPEAL TO YOUNG NONCONFORMISTS. Five Papers. By R. F. HORTON, Hampstead. Price 2d. 12s. per 100.

A QUIET DAY FOR MINISTERS IN MANCHESTER. By Rev. S. HARTLEY. An Address delivered in Besses Congregational Church, Prestwich. Price 1d. 6s. per 100.

WHAT IS A CHRISTIAN CHURCH, AND WHY SHOULD I JOIN ONE. By ERIC A. LAWRENCE. Price 2d.

THE NEEDS OF YOUNG MEN. By Archdeacon FARRAR. Paper, 1d. ; or 3s. per 100.

PUBLIC MORALITY. By VOX CLAMANTIS. Reprinted in pamphlet form from THE CHRISTIAN WORLD. 1. BETTING AND GAMBLING—2. OUR STREETS—3. OUR AMUSEMENTS—4. DRINK—5. THE GETTING AND SPENDING OF MONEY. One Penny each, or 3s. per 100.

THREE SERMONS BY DR. CLIFFORD.

THE PULPIT AND HUMAN LIFE ; or, the Minister as the Interpreter and Spiritual Leader of Human Life. An Address delivered to the Students of the Lancashire Independent College, Manchester. Price Twopence.

THE OLD TESTAMENT IN THE TEACHING OF JESUS. A Sermon preached at the Annual Meetings of the Baptist Churches of the Midland Association, held at Wolverhampton. Price Twopence.

COMING THEOLOGY. By J. CLIFFORD, M.A., D.D. Second Edition. An Address from the Chair of the General Baptist Association. Price 3d.

Biblical and Religious.

THE EPIC OF THE INNER LIFE, BEING THE BOOK OF JOB Translated Anew, and Accompanied with Notes and an Introduction Study. By JOHN F. GENUNG. Price 4s. net.

SERVICE IN THREE CITIES. Twenty-five years' Christian Ministry. By S. PEARSON, M.A. Price 2s. 6d.

A POPULAR ARGUMENT FOR THE UNITY OF ISAIAH. With an Examination of the Opinions of Canons Cheyne and Driver, Dr. Delitzsch, the Rev. G. A. Smith, and others. By JOHN KENNEDY, M.A., D.D. Price 2s. 6d.

THE SCHOOL OF LIFE. Bible Pictures from the Book of Jonah. By OTTO FUNCKE. Second Edition, price 3s.

WHO WROTE THE BIBLE? A Book for the People. By WASHINGTON GLADDEN. Price 4s.

THE INSPIRED BOOK AND THE PERFECT MAN. By Z. MATHER. Price 1s.

INTERNATIONAL CONGREGATIONAL COUNCIL REPORT, London 1891. Being a Report of the Proceedings. Portraits and Views. Royal 8vo, price 5s.

INSPIRATION AND INERRANCY. By C. A. BRIGGS, D.D., LLEWELLYN J. EVANS, D.D., HENRY PRESERVED SMITH, D.D. With an Introduction by ALEXANDER BALMAIN BRUCE, D.D. Price 3s. 6d.

MEMOIR OF AND SERMONS by the late Dr. STEVENSON, Brixton. *In the Press.* Price 3s. 6d.

LOYALTY TO CHRIST. By JOHN PULSFORD, D.D. 7s. 6d.

THE RIGHT AND WRONG USES OF THE BIBLE. New Edition. By R. HEBER NEWTON, Rector of All Souls' Church, New York. Crown 8vo, cloth, 3s. 6d.

THYSELF AND OTHERS. Six Chapters on Practical Christianity. By Rev. SAMUEL PEARSON, M.A., Minister of Highbury Quadrant Church. Cloth 16mo, 1s.

A FRIEND OF MISSIONS IN INDIA. Being the Journal kept by Dr. LUNN when in that country. 1s.

MANSFIELD COLLEGE. A Record of the Opening Ceremony, together with a History of the Foundation. With Six Drawings, on plate paper, of the interior and exterior of the buildings. Medium 8vo, handsome cloth binding, 10s. 6d.

NEW POINTS TO OLD TEXTS. By Rev. JAMES M. WHITON, Ph.D., Author of "Summer Sermons," "The Law of Liberty," &c., &c. Crown 8vo, cloth, 3s. 6d.

BURNING QUESTIONS. By WASHINGTON GLADDEN, D.D., Author of "Things New and Old." Second Edition. Crown 8vo, cloth, 3s. 6d.

QUESTIONS FOR THE FREE CHURCHES. By Rev. J. BRIERLEY, B.A. A Series of Papers reprinted from THE CHRISTIAN WORLD. Crown 8vo, cloth, 2s. 6d.

THE FREEDOM OF FAITH. By Rev. T. T. MUNGER. Sixth Edition. Crown 8vo, 3s. 6d.

EARLY PUPILS OF THE SPIRIT. By JAMES M. WHITON, Ph.D. Crown 8vo, paper, 6d.

WHAT OF SAMUEL? By JAMES M. WHITON, Ph.D. Crown 8vo, paper cover, 1s.

BEYOND THE SHADOW. By JAMES M. WHITON, Ph.D. Third Thousand. Crown 8vo, cloth, 3s. 6d.

SCIENCE AND THE SPIRITUAL. By Prof. A. J Du Bois. Author of "Science and the Supernatural." Sewed, 6d.

HENRY WARD BEECHER IN ENGLAND: A MEMORIAL VOLUME. Consisting of SERMONS, PRAYERS, LECTURES, and ADDRESSES, together with A BIOGRAPHICAL SKETCH and PHOTOGRAPHIC PORTRAIT. Crown 8vo, cloth, 5s.

HENRY WARD BEECHER'S PRAYERS IN THE CONGREGATION. Crown 8vo, 4s. 6d.

HENRY WARD BEECHER'S LAST SERMONS. Sermons delivered at Plymouth Church after Mr. Beecher's return from England. Crown 8vo, cloth, 3s. 6d.

HENRY WARD BEECHER'S RELIGION AND DUTY. Fifty-Two Sunday Readings. Selected by Rev. J. REEVES BROWN. Crown 8vo, cloth, 3s. 6d.

THE SCRIPTURES, HEBREW AND CHRISTIAN. By EDWARD T. BARTLETT, A.M., and JOHN P. PETERS, Ph.D. To be completed in Three Volumes. Vol. II., now ready, 7s. 6d. A handsome, strongly-bound volume of over 500 pages.

A DAY WITH CHRIST. By Rev. SAMUEL COX, D.D. New Edition. 2s. 6d.

THE BEAUTIFUL GLEANER. A Hebrew Pastoral Story: being Familiar Expositions of the Book of Ruth. By the late Rev. WILLIAM BRADEN. Third Edition. Crown 8vo, cloth, gilt edges, 2s. 6d.

OUR PRINCIPLES. A CHURCH MANUAL FOR CONGREGATIONALISTS. By Rev. G. B. JOHNSON. Fifth Edition. 6d.

AIDS TO PUBLIC PRAYER. By Rev. AMBROSE D. SPONG. 1s.

GATHERINGS FROM THE WRITINGS OF THE LATE REV. T. T. LYNCH. Crown 8vo, cloth, 2s. 6d. Second Series.

General.

WHY I LEFT CONGREGATIONALISM. By Rev. GEORGE SALE REANEY. 1s.

THE ART OF AUTHORSHIP: LITERARY REMINISCENCES, METHODS OF WORK, AND ADVICE TO YOUNG BEGINNERS. Personally contributed in illustration of the art of effective written composition by the Leading Authors of the Day. Compiled and Edited by Rev. GEORGE BAINTON. Crown 8vo, cloth, 5s.

TITHES: THEIR HISTORY, USE, AND FUTURE. By R. L. EVERETT, late M.P. for Woodbridge Division of Suffolk. Second Edition. Crown 8vo, paper, 6d.

NINETIETH THOUSAND.

TASTY DISHES, Showing what we can have for Breakfast, Dinner, Tea, and Supper. Crown 8vo, 1s.

A Wedding Present or Gift-Book to Young Married People.

THE HOME: IN ITS RELATION TO MAN AND TO SOCIETY. By late Rev. JAMES BALDWIN BROWN. Crown 8vo, cloth, 3s. 6d. In handsome Calf or Morocco binding, 10s. 6d.

HOMELY TALKS ABOUT HOMELY THINGS. By MARIANNE FARNINGHAM. Foolscap 8vo, cloth, 2s. 6d.

LIFE SKETCHES AND ECHOES FROM THE VALLEY. By MARIANNE FARNINGHAM. Each crown 8vo, cloth, 2s. 6d. ; gilt edges, 3s.

WHAT SHALL WE NAME IT? A Dictionary of Baptismal Names for Children. Containing 2,000 names, with their meaning and the countries from which they originated. 6d.

Poetry.

BY MARIANNE FARNINGHAM.

GILBERT AND OTHER POEMS. By MARIANNE FARN-
INGHAM. Third Edition. Fcap. 8vo, extra cloth, 3s. 6d. ;
gilt edges, 4s.

LAYS AND LYRICS OF THE BLESSED LIFE. By
MARIANNE FARNINGHAM. Eighth Thousand. Revised
edition. Crown 8vo, cloth, 2s. 6d. ; gilt edges, 3s.

LEAVES FROM ELIM : POEMS. By MARIANNE FARN-
INGHAM. Third Thousand. Crown 8vo, cloth, 4s. ; gilt
edges, 4s. 6d.

SONGS OF SUNSHINE : The Newest Volume of Poems
by MARIANNE FARNINGHAM. Second Thousand. Crown
8vo, cloth, 4s.

For Young People.

DIALOGUES FOR SCHOOL AND HOME. By Rev. H.
J. HARVEY. A companion book to the "Reedham Dialogues."
Imperial 32mo, cloth, 1s.

BOYHOOD : A COLLECTION OF FORTY PAPERS ON BOYS
AND THEIR WAYS. By MARIANNE FARNINGHAM. Eighth
Thousand. Fcap. 8vo, 1s. 6d. ; gilt edges, 2s.

BYE-PATH MEADOW. By late Rev. E. PAXTON HOOD.
Fcap. 8vo, cloth, 3s. 6d.

CHILDREN'S HOLIDAYS. By MARIANNE FARNINGHAM. 1s.

THE CLARENCE FAMILY ; or, Brothers and Sisters.
By MARIANNE FARNINGHAM. Fcap. 8vo, cloth, 1s. 6d. ;
gilt edges, 2s.

GIRLHOOD. By MARIANNE FARNINGHAM. Twentieth
Thousand. Fcap. 8vo, cloth, 1s. 6d. ; gilt edges, 2s.

HOME LIFE : TWENTY-NINE PAPERS ON FAMILY MATTERS.
By MARIANNE FARNINGHAM. A Companion Volume to
"Girlhood." Eighth Thousand. Fcap. 8vo, cloth, 1s. 6d. ;
gilt edges, 2s.

LITTLE TALES FOR LITTLE READERS. A Book for the
Little Ones. By MARIANNE FARNINGHAM. Uniform with
"Girlhood," "Boyhood," and "Home Life." Fcap. 8vo,
cloth, 1s. 6d. ; gilt edges, 2s.

THE MORAL PIRATES, AND THE CRUISE OF "THE GHOST." With TWENTY-FIVE ILLUSTRATIONS. By W. L. ALDEN. Crown 8vo, cloth, 2s. 6d.

REEDHAM DIALOGUES. A Dozen Dialogues for Children. By late JOHN EDMED, Head Master of the Asylum for Fatherless Children, Reedham, Croydon. Eighth Thousand. Imperial 32mo, cloth, 1s. 6d.

WHAT OF THE NIGHT? A Temperance Tale of the Times. By MARIANNE FARNINGHAM. Fourth Thousand. Crown 8vo, Illuminated Cover, 1s.

THE BABY'S ANNUAL.

THE ROSEBUD ANNUAL FOR 1892. The Twelve Monthly Numbers of *The Rosebud*. In handsome cloth binding. Nearly 300 charming illustrations. Quarto, 4s.

DAILY CHRONICLE: "*The genial humour in which children take such delight distinguishes a large number of the tales, sketches, and rhymes; and the illustrations, which reach a total of nearly three hundred, possess exceptional merit.*"

PRESTON GUARDIAN: "*To many homes this book comes as a yearly visitor eagerly looked for by the children, whose expectations this year we are sure will be more than realised.*"

One Volume Novels.

A MAN'S MISTAKE. By MINNIE WORBOISE. Crown 8vo, cloth, 5s.

ALL HE KNEW. A religious Novel. By JOHN HABBERTON, Author of "Helen's Babies," &c. Crown 8vo, cloth, 2s. 6d.

ROSLYN'S TRUST. By LUCY C. LILLIE, Author of "Prudence," "Kenyon's Wife," "The Household of Glen Holly." Crown 8vo, cloth, 3s. 6d.

"*I have seldom, if ever, read a work of fiction that moved me with so much admiration.*"—GEORGE MACDONALD.

FOR THE RIGHT: A GERMAN ROMANCE. By EMIL FRANZOS. Given in English by JULIE SUTTER (translator of "Letters from Hell"). Preface by Dr. GEORGE MACDONALD. Crown 8vo, cloth, 3s. 6d. Third Edition.

DINAH'S SON. By L. B. WALFORD. Crown 8vo, cloth, 3s. 6d.

HAGAR: A NORTH YORKSHIRE STORY. By MARY LINSKILL, Author of "Between the Heather and the Northern Sea," "The Haven under the Hill," &c., &c. Crown 8vo, 1s.

LILLO AND RUTH; or, Aspirations. By HELEN HAYS.
Crown 8vo, cloth, 3s. 6d.

MERTONSVILLE PARK; OR, HERBERT SEYMOUR'S CHOICE.
By Mrs. WOODWARD. Fifth Edition. Crown 8vo, cloth, 5s.

CLARISSA'S TANGLED WEB. By BEATRICE BRISTOWE.
Crown 8vo, cloth, 5s.

SISTER URSULA. By LUCY WARDEN BEARNE. Crown
8vo, cloth, 5s.

PRISCILLA; OR, THE STORY OF A BOY'S LOVE. By CLARA
L. WILLMETS. Cloth, 1s. 6d.

THE CATHEDRAL SHADOW. By MARIANNE FARN-
INGHAM. Fifth Thousand. Crown 8vo, cloth, 3s. 6d.; gilt
edges, 4s.

THE SNOW QUEEN. By MAGGIE SYMINGTON. Third
Thousand. Fcap. 8vo, cloth, 1s 6d.; gilt edges, 2s.

BY AMELIA E. BARR.

"Mrs. Barr's stories are always pleasant to read. They are full of sweetness
and light."—SCOTSMAN.

"In descriptive writing, in simplicity and gracefulness of style, and in perfect
mastery over her characters, Mrs. Barr can hold her own with any living English
novelist."—GLASGOW HERALD.

NOW READY.

FRIEND OLIVIA. Crown 8vo, 6s.

In a variety of handsome cloth bindings, or bound uniformly, crown 8vo.
THREE SHILLINGS AND SIXPENCE EACH.

In the Press. A SISTER TO ESAU.

SHE LOVED A SAILOR.	IN SPITE OF HIMSELF
Just Ready	A BORDER SHEPHERDESS
THE LAST OF THE MAC-	PAUL AND CHRISTINA
ALLISTERS.	THE SQUIRE OF SANDAL SIDE
WOVEN OF LOVE AND GLORY	THE BOW OF ORANGE RIBBON
FEET OF CLAY (*with portrait*	BETWEEN TWO LOVES
of author)	A DAUGHTER OF FIFE
THE HOUSEHOLD OF McNEIL	JAN VEDDER'S WIFE

*** *A new and cheap edition of* "JAN VEDDER'S WIFE" *is now
issued. In paper cover, price 1s. 6d.*

THE HARVEST OF THE WIND, AND OTHER STORIES.
By AMELIA E. BARR. Crown 8vo, paper, 1s.

NOVELS BY EMMA JANE WORBOISE.
NEW AND CHEAP EDITION.

*** *These Novels, which have hitherto been sold at Five Shillings*
each, are now issued at

THREE SHILLINGS AND SIXPENCE EACH.

Thornycroft Hall
Millicent Kendrick
St. Beetha's
Violet Vaughan
Margaret Torrington
The Fortunes of Cyril Denham
Singlehurst Manor
Overdale
Grey and Gold
Mr. Montmorency's Money
Nobly Born
Chrystabel
Canonbury Holt
Husbands and Wives
The House of Bondage
Emilia's Inheritance

Father Fabian
Oliver Westwood
Lady Clarissa
Grey House at Endlestone
Robert Wreford's Daughter
The Brudenells of Brude
The Heirs of Errington
Joan Carisbroke
A Woman's Patience
The Story of Penelope
Sissie
The Abbey Mill
Warleigh's Trust
Esther Wynne
Fortune's Favourite
His Next of Kin.

The following 3s. 6d. Volumes are now issued at Three Shillings each.

Married Life ; or, The Story of Phillip and Edith.
Our New House ; or, Keeping up Appearances.
Heartsease in the Family
Maude Bolingbroke

Amy Wilton
Helen Bury

BOOKS FOR THE HOLIDAYS. SPECIAL OFFER.

A limited number of the following Novels, published at Four Shillings and Sixpence, are now offered at Two Shillings and Sixpence.

Campion Court
Evelyn's Story
Lottie Lonsdale

Sir Julian's Wife
The Lillingstones
The Wife's Trials

www.ingramcontent.com/pod-product-compliance
Lightning Source LLC
Chambersburg PA
CBHW020849020726
47497CB00005B/1333